SHELL

A Novel

CHRIS GILL

PRNTD

Published by PRNTD Publishing 2015

3 4 5 7 9 10 8 6 4 2

Copyright © Chris Gill 2015

Chris Gill asserts the moral right to
be identified as the author of this work

ISBN 9780994462008

This novel is entirely a work of fiction.
The names, characters and incidents portrayed in it are
the work of the author's imagination. Any resemblance to
actual persons, living or dead, events or localities is
entirely coincidental.

All rights reserved. No part of this book may be
reproduced, stored in a retrieval system, or transmitted
in any form, by any means, including mechanical,
electric, photocopying, recording or otherwise, without the prior
written permission of the publisher.

First published in Australia in 2015 by PRNTD Publishing

Typeset in Baskerville

www.prntdpublishing.com

For Michael

"The sea, once it casts its spell, holds one in its net of wonder forever."

— Jacques Yves Cousteau

PROLOGUE

Like crystals scattered over a powder-blue blanket. That's what came to the young girl's mind the very first time she saw the ocean. The way the sun glistened upon the crashing waves reminded her instantly of the little sparkly wonders her mother finished her outfit off with when she was dressing up for the evening.

Her mother looked so beautiful when she was dressed up. Just like the ocean. It wasn't that she didn't look beautiful all the time. There was just something extra special about those crystals. How they glimmered in the light. It was as if they illuminated her whole presence.

The girl's second earliest memory of the ocean was when she was sat with her mother, surrounded by shells on the beach. She couldn't have been much older than five. Her red locks hung down against her freckled cheeks as she looked up into her mother's warm almond eyes.

"If you hold it up against your ear, you can hear the entire ocean," her mother said softly, looking straight back down at her daughter. The young girl picked up the large conch and raised it towards her head. Delicate coils spiralled intricately around its pearlescent cave with splashes of pink and amber.

The girl held the shell's opening to her ear, closed her eyes and listened…

Four years later, the Old World was destroyed.

PART ONE

SURFACE TO AIR

ONE

As Red stepped out of the nightclub, she felt the artificial rain lightly touching her skin. Slowly walking away from the throbbing sound behind her, she pulled her black hood over her toxic green denim jacket and lit a cigarette. While she understood how necessary the rain was, she was always so conscious of how unnatural it felt when it made contact with her. Like she was a piece of genetically-modified fruit soaked in pesticides.

The young woman's gold knee-length platform boots stomped noisily over the bumps and rusty coils in the pavement as she walked away from the club. It was always so much worse on this part of town. As if she was literally walking along the surface of the Reactor. If she'd pressed her ear against the ground, she would have heard its distinctive monotone humming through the layers of metal.

The thumping beat grew quieter and quieter until it disappeared completely. It was always the same thing with that place, or perhaps it was just that she'd grown tired of that scene. She'd been surrounded by hedonism since her early teens and was no stranger to the darkest corners of life and the most dangerous kinds of people. Maybe it was after chasing too many thrills that the novelty of reckless living had finally worn off. Maybe she'd simply grown up.

Red stamped her cigarette out on the ground beneath her boot, before turning another street corner into an even darker and narrower alleyway. The government would imitate the day and night system that had existed in the Old World by switching the lights on and off. Although Red understood this was necessary for growing crops and aiding people's sleeping patterns, she still disagreed with it. *Wouldn't it feel a hell of a lot safer for a young girl walking home on her own in the middle of the night if the lights were just left on all the time?*

Red's thoughts were interrupted as she stumbled over something soft below her boots and fell onto the side of the pavement. The cat let out a piercing scream as it backed away from her.

"Shit!" Red got halfway back up, then moved towards the small black feline that she'd unexpectedly awoken. "I'm sorry precious, come over here. Why are you all alone on a night like this? Don't you have a home?"

Her warm, velvety tone was enough to reassure the animal that she wasn't a threat. The cat cautiously allowed the stranger to move in closer and check the small metallic chip that was attached to her neck. Red pressed the chip's surface before a blurry three-dimensional hologram of an elderly woman projected above the animal. The entire alleyway lit up.

"Have you found Aura? Please return her to Level…" As the cat's owner began to read out her address, the recording flickered twice then went out completely as the chip lost all power. Red tapped it a few more times, but to no avail.

"Well, Aura," Red said, scooping her new-found companion up into her arms. "Looks like you're stuck with me now until you remember your way home."

The young woman had only walked a few steps further down the alleyway with Aura tightly in her grasp before she heard the first man speak.

"Here, kitty kitty kitty. Here, kitty kitty kitty," The man's voice was soft and high, but full of malice. Red kept on walking but picked up the pace, only to be greeted by another man who was in front of her this time.

"What's the rush lil' lady, don't you wanna have a kiss in the rain?" The man behind her continued to approach making kissing sounds in the air.

"How romantic. Wouldn't that be romantic, little kitty?" Red sensed that he was the leader of the pair and was probably more dangerous.

"Look guys, I really don't want any trouble. My cat and I are just walking home and want to be left alone." Red was trying her best to cover any signs of fear in her voice as she stared into the eyes of her opposition.

His dark curly hair was soaked from the rain, dripping over his sullen grey eyes. His nose ring moved up and down as his nostrils flared. There was something intimidating about the rips in his faded denim jacket. She couldn't help but visualise the women who had torn it in an attempt to keep him off.

"Well, maybe we don't want to leave you alone," the voice behind continued as the man in front pushed Red backwards into his accomplice's arms.

Aura leapt out of her grasp onto the dirty street and let out a piercing screech. It was in this brief moment that Red's thoughts shot back to the nightclub she'd just left and how, like always, she'd chosen not to listen to the advice of her friend and flatmate. Delta, although never one to turn down a good time, was without a doubt the sensible one of the two and constantly worried for Red's welfare.

"Just stick around for another half an hour or so, Xave and I will be leaving too. That way we can all grab a pod home." Red remembered Delta's exact words, but ignored them completely. Her strong mind would often be mistaken for stubbornness, and tonight would be no exception.

"It's fine, I'm going to walk. I could do with the air, if you can even call it that." Red had finished her drink and started to make her way across the crowded dance floor to the exit.

"At least let me order you a pod. I don't want you walking home alone again, it's not safe!" As always, Delta's words were spoken in vain. Red knew her friend was right. It wasn't safe. Particularly on this side of the city where nineteen-year-olds went to nightclubs. The streets were considered to be even less safe now that humanity existed under the ocean.

The seacity, which had been worked on for years in preparation for disaster, had been turned into a crime-filled hellhole with more problems than the world above had ever known. Despite threats by the Authorities to keep theft, violence and murders down, they never seemed to be around to enforce the law. They never seemed to show up when they were actually needed. They didn't show up on the night Red was attacked on her way home.

"Get off me! Somebody help!" Red's screaming only encouraged the two men more as they forcefully restrained her from kicking and shoving. The eldest of the pair stepped in front of her and pulled up the sleeves of his ripped denim jacket to reveal an angel tattooed on his forearm.

"No need to make a scene now, is there sweetheart?" His hollow face forced a grimace that made Red's stomach turn. "It's always the redheads, eh Taylor? Feisty ain't they?"

As Taylor kept Red's arms locked tightly behind her back and pulled her to the ground, she watched the angel on the stranger's arm move closer towards her as he reached in, pushing his hand down her tights and in between her legs.

The next minute flew past in an instant as Red pulled back her leg and released it forward in a powerful blow. The platform of her boot was sent thrusting into her attacker's face, bursting it open and sending a gush of blood spraying out onto the ground. The man let out a painful howl and grabbed onto his broken nose as Taylor, the more timid of the two, let go of her and ran. Red then pulled a switchblade out from the inside of her boot and pointed it directly towards the lone remaining man.

"This redhead is far feistier than you realised."

With that, the bloodied stranger went from monster to mouse and scampered away into the night. Red stood up and brushed the dirt off of her lean figure as she stuffed the switchblade back into her boot. The rain began to subside before she removed her hood, shaking a thick mane of long fire-red hair. Aura cautiously reappeared with tiny silent steps from around the corner.

"Good thing our lives aren't in your hands, hey Aura? Then again, you do have nine of them to throw around." She scooped the cat up into her arms and continued journeying towards her flat. One thing that Red had learned over the years was how to always find her way back home alone. But on this night, she didn't mind the company at all.

TWO

Red could make out the silhouette of an angel she'd seen many times before. She knew its familiar form, as always, but she couldn't see its face. As she moved forward, she noticed that the majestic being was covering something. Before she had a chance to remember what it was, the roots of a tree pushed past the angel's wings and wrapped themselves around her.

Red looked up and saw the Four Horsemen of the Apocalypse riding through the clouds disguised as Authorities, with the Grim Reaper in the lead. He pulled out a sword and began to slay the tree's branches and the angel's wings. Red opened her mouth to scream but nothing came out. The angel looked up in agony and stared into her daughter's eyes.

Red jolted upright bathed in sweat, breathing heavily. The sudden movement prompted Aura to leap from the bed to the room's cold metallic floor. Red switched on her industrial bedside light, took a deep breath and looked at the time: *08:06*.

The cat hissed with annoyance before curling up underneath the bed.

"Sorry, sweetheart," she whispered softly to her new pet. This was the third week in a row that Red had woken from the same dream. She lay in silence for five minutes or so before the front door buzzed. Still half asleep, she climbed out of her stiff white sheets and got dressed for work.

Most people in the United Underworld, or *The Shell* as its inhabitants dubbed it, worked at the Reactor, where they wore the same uniform in a clinical mint hue. The Authorities dressed in white while therapists and paramedics dressed in slate grey. Red was one of the lucky ones who had managed to avoid the system's plan for her and worked in an underground bookstore. Despite being technically illegal, it posed no real threat and kept someone like Red quiet. She dressed to suit her mood.

These were the only real options for work in The Shell. Everyone else roamed the streets and stole whatever they could get their hands on. The ones who were caught by Authorities were shot on the spot with a raygun without a second thought. There were no trials in The Shell.

Red made her way to the door in a sheer black dress, smoothing her ruby locks back so they were out of her face. She knew the walk so well that she could probably do it with her eyes closed, even in her trademark platform boots. Six steps to the hallway and four more to the right. Then she would scoop her heightened five-foot frame a little as she approached the door.

Everybody lived in the same style of flats in The Shell.

Cramped corridors with even tinier rooms and only the most basic of amenities made up the personal living spaces that were usually shared. Every block had ten flats on all of its twenty levels, each with a unique code.

"Who is it?" she asked peering through the peephole. A handsome man with sky-blue eyes and a shaved head looked back at her. All men who worked for the government were made to shave off their hair, while women tied theirs back, symbolising a united front. In Red's eyes, this just kept people from expressing their personalities.

"Hi Red. My name's Ethan and I'll be working with you from now on," he spoke quickly but with a friendly tone, dressed in the standard grey uniform all therapists wore.

"I'm not interested in what you have to say. Please leave," Red spoke sternly as she turned her back on the door. "Besides, I'm already late for work."

After it became clear to the government that the people of The Shell were finding it difficult to settle into their landless lives, they introduced a law for all citizens above the age of twelve to have weekly therapy sessions. It was a way of helping people deal with their new lives in the United Underworld, as well as helping them cope with their losses.

Despite his persistence, Red had never opened up to her previous therapist. He would visit every Saturday morning for an hour's session of *mind games,* as she called them. Delta, on the other hand, found herself effortlessly talking to her therapist. Then again, Red often mocked Delta for talking to anyone willing to listen.

"Look Red, I'm not here to interrogate you," Ethan

persisted. "I'm just here to get to know a little bit more about you and find out how you're… coping with everything. I promise I won't stay long."

"Everything you know about me already, doctor, is all you're ever going to know." Red left the therapist waiting at the door as she headed back to her room to grab her beaten-up old rucksack.

Aura had curled back up inside of Red's bed sheets like a furry snail shell.

"You have no idea how envious I am of you right now," Red said with a coy conviction.

She then headed back to her front door and noticed that a small piece of paper had been slipped underneath.

I'll try again later. Have a great day. E.

Red rolled her eyes, screwed the piece of paper up and threw it across the room, straight into the recycling shoot. She really was going to be late.

Red's distressed black platform boots stomped noisily across the dusty metallic street as she headed towards work. Her bookstore was hidden away in a quiet part of the city that Authorities rarely bothered with. There was nothing else surrounding her store except for a few boarded up buildings and a junkyard.

Despite its setting, it was surprising how busy the shop could get sometimes. This meant that Red tried to have it open by at least 10:00 every morning. After the Digital Age had consumed the need for print entirely, bookstores became almost obsolete in the twenty-second century. Nevertheless, Red found herself with a loyal customer base. Like her, these customers adored literature and would travel from the other side of the city to bring in books from their own collections and purchase new ones.

Books were scarce in The Shell, as most of them had been destroyed in the Apocalypse. They existed predominantly on the black market, which is what made Red's store so unique. It had led to the young woman becoming a collector and she'd do everything in her power to get her hands on as many books as she could find.

Red had stumbled across the abandoned building on her seventeenth birthday. She'd attended a rave there with a group of friends when the idea hatched inside her ecstasy-filled mind to transform the warehouse into her very own bookstore. The next morning, despite a throbbing headache and awful comedown, Red carried her personal collection of books to the derelict building before piling them across offcuts of fabric. She scrawled paragraphs from her favourite books across the walls of the shop and encouraged her customers to do the same when they visited.

Red sat down and unfolded her wafer-thin computer. With the touch of her fingertip, she instantly logged into the UUW (United Underworld Web), the online system that the citizens of The Shell used. It was similar to the Internet system that had been used in the Old World, but it had several limitations. All social networking websites were censored and any sort of news reporting was banned. These restrictions furthered Red's distrust towards the government, as she felt the nation was being kept in the dark as to why developments were lingering above the ground.

Red gently scrolled her finger down the screen to check her inbox, although she'd already checked it on her connector on her way to work. Nothing. No mail. No change. Along the top of the screen in large text read the sentence: UNITED UNDERWORLD WEB SERVICE PROVIDED BY YOUR SECRETARY OF STATE AND LEADER, PRESIDENT IVAN SPENCER. Red scowled at the words and felt her blood heat up just thinking about him. No one seemed to understand her suspicions of Ivan Spencer. She often offended those who saw him as their saviour when the Old World had been destroyed. He'd not only given humanity a second chance of life, but also hope that one day the world they'd once taken for granted would be rebuilt.

It was a decade before the asteroid hit that Ivan Spencer became England's leader. Red had grown up seeing the hologram of his angular face under a glow of wispy white hair. Even as a child she would giggle and mimic the way he spoke to the country with aggression and self-assurance, despite not understanding the words he would spit at the time.

His father, Jonathan Spencer, had been leader for over thirty years before his death and had been made famous for controversially abolishing the British Monarchy. He'd also begun working on what he called the *Underworld*, which was a large city underneath the ocean that would one day be used for refuge from man-made or natural disaster. Although he began to do this on the seabed of the Atlantic, he hoped that the whole world would eventually join him with this ambitious development.

After Jonathan Spencer's death, his son became leader and

swore to follow in his father's footsteps by finishing the Underworld. As technology became more advanced, he worked quicker and more effectively on the vast project, continuing what Jonathan Spencer had started. The seacity would accommodate the entire population of England.

Encased in an enormous pebble-shaped vat, it would remain unsecured to the bottom of the ocean, floating and using the seawater itself as insulation from disaster. Its walls constructed from indestructibly-strong alloys.

The seacity was eventually completed and revealed to the public, branded as the *United* Underworld. Ivan Spencer had proposed a global expansion plan to other world leaders but his failed attempt left The Shell the only structure of its kind.

Within hours after the asteroid was first spotted heading towards Earth by astronomers, citizens were already preparing to board giant vessels that would transport them to their new home and sanctuary from the impending catastrophe above. Ivan Spencer made a vow to the nation that while they existed over three thousand metres beneath the sea, he would use his advanced technology to rebuild the Old World so that one day humanity could set foot in daylight and fresh air once more.

"Get off that piece of nonsense and stick this under your nose instead!" Marcus Moore's worn-out voice was warm, familiar and enough to replace Red's gloomy expression with the widest smile imaginable.

"Why would you choose to spend your time on that thing when you're surrounded by so many beautiful books?"

Red squealed in delight as she leapt out from behind her screen and threw her arms around her old friend. Marcus was one of the most kind-hearted and gentle people she'd ever met. In many ways, she saw him as the grandfather she'd never known. Despite being in his eighties, he had a spring in his step and his memories all intact. This was no real surprise in an age where life expectancy was as high as 110 years. The only real problem he appeared to have was a raspy cough that interrupted his speech from time to time.

"You need to get that checked out. It sounds like it's getting worse." Red stared into the elderly man's eyes with concern.

"Oh don't worry about me, I feel fantastic!" Marcus pulled out a large fabric bag full of old books, which he laid out on the shop counter. As he did this, a dust cloud softly soared from the bag like a balloon being set free into the air.

"Now this is the sort of thing you ought to be filling that brilliant mind of yours with, my dear." He started shuffling through the literature laid out on the counter, searching for a specific title.

"I don't doubt that, you look great." Red continued, ignoring his advice. "It's just you've had this cough for a while now and I'm worried that—"

"Well don't worry your sweet head, my dear," Marcus interrupted the concerned young woman as he found the book he was looking for.

"Ah yes, here we are. I thought you might enjoy reading this one." He passed her a tatty-looking book titled *The Most Famous Conspiracy Theories of the 21st Century.*

"Besides, I already know why I have this cough. And whatever medication they give me will be nothing in comparison to a deep breath of fresh air from the outside world." He looked up as if he could see through to the clouds in the sky. This prompted Red to do the same as she silently agreed.

In the few areas of The Shell's partly-transparent dome that allowed citizens to see outside, they could usually only see murky water in an inky hue. The impact of the asteroid might not have been enough to destroy the oceans, but its gasses and subsequent meteor showers had poisoned them, leaving an inhospitable environment.

Dead fish, sharks, dolphins, jellyfish and even whales would drift by The Shell, motionless and skeletal. Occasionally a living creature would swim by bringing an instant smile to the onlooker's face. Like a rare bird flying across the sky of the Old World.

"I just don't understand why they haven't started rebuilding yet." Red's words were uttered in bewilderment as she looked back down at the book of controversial theories in front of her. "They say it's the toxic fumes the asteroid left behind but I know it's just they don't want to spend any money. It's always about money."

"You're never going to give up fighting the machine, are you my dear?" Marcus looked at his young friend with pride as Red answered him with determination in her eyes.

THREE

It was exactly 17:00 when Professor Prothero realised that he hadn't slept for over twenty-four hours. He'd been so carried away with his experiments that he'd completely lost track of time. This was until he noticed that the light outside his window had gone from off to on and then off again. The scientist sat down for a moment, realising how exhausted he was.

He looked up and noticed that all the crops he was growing started to change colour. The plants went from green to blue to red to black. He then watched in terror as the crops began to grow bigger and bigger and finally start moving towards him, closer and closer until the vines were reaching out for his throat…

Prothero awoke from his dream abruptly and gasped out loud for air. He looked around the laboratory at the crops he was testing and realised that they were still green and their usual size. Feeling no less unsettled, the scientist leapt up from his chair to continue his analysis through yet another night.

* * *

As Delta left for work, she ran her left hand through her curly brown locks and eyed up the pod bay opposite to find her boyfriend. Like clockwork, Xavier was sitting in his vehicle waiting for her to finish with a huge grin on his face. The pair had only been dating for a few months, but they were already head over heels in love.

Like most men in The Shell, Xavier worked as a mechatronic engineer. This meant he kept on top of the complex structures that made up the United Underworld, most notably the Reactor.

The Reactor was a series of colossal tanks, hydroelectric turbines and a giant generator built to convert the sea's current into electricity, ultimately powering The Shell. It was so heavily integrated into the United Underworld that you could hear the turbines spinning from almost anywhere in the seacity. It controlled the day and night lighting system, provided citizens with clean drinking water and released artificial rain to help the crops grow.

Delta got into the pod and kissed her lover on the lips before releasing a long sigh of exhaustion. "I had the worst hangover all day. I don't know how I managed to get anything done!" Delta, like most women in The Shell, worked on a different part of the Reactor where she carried out maintenance checks, as well as cleaning duties.

"Tell me about it," Xavier said. "I could hardly focus on the system I was working on today." The handsome young man quickly entered their destination and the pod accelerated along the frictionless magnetic rails below in an attempt to miss the chaotic rush of rail traffic that would follow.

Pods made up The Shell's transport system. They tended to be the same slate grey colour and were shaped like large moving eggs that were just big enough for two people to sit upright in. Some were akin to taxis in the Old World and others were privately owned, mostly by people who worked for the government.

"Did you see Red at all when we got in last night?" Xavier continued, scratching the side of his shaved head. His hair had been a golden hue as a child, but was now far darker due to the lack of sunlight. "I'm sorry I passed out straight away, that pod went the long way home and I was dead beat. I swear we programmed it to go the other way."

"Well, I saw her gold boots dumped in the hallway outside her room but I decided not to wake her." Delta felt squeamish as the pod sped through the dusty streets. "I worry about that girl so much, Xave. I mean, I know she's got a lot of opinions. But she walks around like she's invincible sometimes. I just don't want to see her get into trouble."

Xavier rolled his eyes in the way he had so many times on the subject. "You know you're not going to change her D, that's the way she is. That girl has got so much anger in there. I've never seen anything like it. But she's tough and can take care of herself." Xavier squeezed his girlfriend's hand reassuringly.

"I know that's the way she is. I've known her for what feels like forever and she's far more behaved now, believe me." Delta smiled to herself knowingly. "I just wish she'd stop obsessing about how much she hates the system all the time. It's like she's brainwashed or something."

Red was already home when the couple walked in. She sat cross-legged on the sofa reading from her thin and transparent connector, a pocket-sized rectangular device that all citizens owned and constantly checked.

Albeit not very big, Red and Delta's flat was comfortable enough and had everything they needed. They'd lived together for years, but Xavier had practically moved in since the two began dating.

"Oh good, you're alive then!" Delta smiled at her friend as she headed towards the kitchen.

"Don't be so dramatic, of course I'm alive," said Red. "Oh and by the way, we have a new roommate, I hope you don't mind." Aura crawled out from underneath Red's book purring loudly. "Her name's Aura, I found her on my way home last night but her chip's broken."

"She's adorable!" Delta said grinning. "Of course I don't mind." She walked over and sat down next to her flatmate. "Although, I guess I already have my pet over all the time."

"I heard that!" Xavier had already collapsed in a heap in Delta's bedroom.

The young women laughed as they sat curled up on the sofa with Aura in the middle.

Red had met Delta four years after the asteroid hit. The Authorities had taken Red to an emergency orphanage where she was raised until she was fifteen. This was the age that people in The Shell were considered adults. Schooling no longer existed in the United Underworld. Instead, young people received vocational training for the limited career options that were available. With no direction or parental figures in her life, Red was completely against the establishment by her teens. She would steal from supermarkets and sneak out of her refuge into nightclubs that she was far too young for. Before the age of fourteen she'd found herself heavily involved with drugs and alcohol, spending each night on a direct path to self-destruction. As far as Red was concerned, her life had no meaning. No purpose.

In many ways, Delta had been Red's saviour, even back then. Delta's background couldn't be more different to Red's, with her parents pushing her enthusiasm and talent for fashion design from an early age. If it hadn't been for the government's request for her to work on the Reactor, she would have pursued a career in making clothes. She would spend every day at home with her mother sewing fabric and filling her sketchbooks. While she enjoyed the creativity, she yearned to meet people her own age. Her parents were obsessively protective, which made it difficult for Delta to make friends.

It had been one of the rare days Delta had been allowed out alone that she'd first set eyes on Red. She had been sent to get fabric from the craft store but had been drawn in by Red's beautiful fragility and mystery as she sat alone on the side of the road. Red had her head in her arms as Delta approached to check if she was okay. In actuality, Red had been upset because a gang of addicts had stolen her gear, but lied and said that she was lost. The two had been inseparable ever since.

Six years on and the two young women sat in the exact same positions on the sofa as they had on the pavement the day they met. Despite the fact that they looked and acted differently, Delta's concern for her friend was as strong as it had been back then.

"Well, at least you weren't completely alone on your way home last night then." Delta picked Aura up into her lap and stroked her head appreciatively.

"That's true. Not that she was any help to me. She scampered off at the first sight of danger–" Red regretted her words as soon as they left her mouth. She'd not planned on telling Delta what had transpired the night before, as she knew exactly how she would react. Delta proved her right.

"I knew it! Something happened, didn't it? Red, I told you that you should have waited for us!" Aura jumped out of Delta's arms as her tone went from soft to stern.

"Delta, please don't start this. I'm a grown up and I can take care of myself. I know what sort of place our world is. I grew up with criminals and junkies, remember? Nothing out there can scare me after seeing the things I've seen." Red got up towards the kitchen and poured herself a large glass of red wine. "That is unless his name is Ivan Spencer, of course. The government's the only monster living under my bed, believe me."

"Oh for the love of God, Red. Can't you just let it go?" Delta got up and walked towards the kitchen, suddenly annoyed. "You spend your life angry at something or someone when you're the one making everything so difficult!" She grabbed the glass out of Red's hand and tipped the wine down the sink. Red defiantly snatched the bottle and poured herself another glass, this time even bigger.

"You know, by trying to act like my mother all the time Delta, you're turning into your own." Red took a sip of the drink before sitting back down.

"Well, turning to that stuff every time you're upset isn't going to bring back yours, is it?" This time it was Delta's turn to regret her words. Red paused briefly before swigging back the entire glass, throwing on her leather jacket and heading towards the door.

"Red, I'm sorry. We're both tired and saying stupid things. I shouldn't have said that…"

Red turned back around to face her friend as she walked out the door. "No, you really shouldn't have."

She slammed the door in Delta's face.

* * *

Red looked up at her mother who was masking her fear with the warmest smile she could muster. She stared back down into her daughter's clear crystal green eyes as the surrounding crowds pushed past. For a moment it was as if time stopped completely as the duo stared at each other wordlessly, until Red finally smiled back at her mother and continued to march ahead. "Don't worry ma, I'm not afraid."

Before they reached the group that Red had been selected to go beneath in, her mother had promised that they would visit her father one last time. They knew they had to move quickly. The fire in the clouds warned that they were running out of time. When they finally reached the copper beech tree they had planted in her father's memory, Red got straight down on her knees and placed her hands gently onto the soil surrounding it. She pulled out a large assortment of yellow roses from her backpack and placed them beside the tree before softly kissing its rippled bark. Although still small, the tree had grown fast. Red knew this was her father's spirit speeding up the process.

Red had never known what her father's favourite flowers had been. If he had any at all. Hers however were yellow roses, so she decided that these were what he would have wanted laid upon him in the world's final moments.

Only seconds after the flowers were placed on the ground, Red's mother lifted her up and began to lead her away. "Come on dear, it's nearly too late."

The pair took one final look back and Red was certain she saw an angel guarding the tree with her wings.

When they reached Red's group, two Authorities swiftly approached them before standing on their sides. Dressed entirely in white with large oval-shaped masks covering their faces, the two men looked almost identical. "Can we have your documents please? You're late."

One of the two men snatched the paper out of Red's mother's hands and quickly scanned them. "Wait here young lady, your mother needs to come with us."

Red looked up at the man and scowled at his unnecessarily brash tone.

"Don't worry officer, my daughter understands that we have to go down separately. Red, I'll be right behind you." She attempted to get down on her knees beside her daughter, but both of the Authorities grabbed Red's mother and forcefully pulled her in a different direction.

"There is no time for goodbyes ma'am, we all have to get down there right away."

Red gasped as she watched her mother being pulled

towards another group by the two strangers.

"I'll meet you down there!" her mother called as she disappeared out of sight.

Unsatisfied with the departure, Red launched forward to follow them before another Authority appeared from the crowds and pulled her into his arms. Like a slow motion scene from a movie, Red found herself being pulled along by the men dressed in white following the rest of the group. Their destination: the departure bay on the beach.

The civilians climbed into countless vessels, each with a capacity to transport one hundred people at a time. They were leaving and arriving at the concrete-covered bay like clockwork. After the Authorities securely buckled Red into her vessel, everyone nervously sat in silence as they were catapulted through the water towards the unknown. Without windows inside the vessel, the group had no idea when they had reached their new world.

People beside Red shook their heads while others cried hysterically. Everyone was pale with fear at the knowledge of what was to come. In this dark moment, the bravery of a nine-year-old girl with hair the colour of the fire in the sky above outweighed that of all the adults who surrounded her. Somewhere deep inside her a flame burned brighter than all of them.

In less than twenty-five minutes, the powerfully-built vessel reached its destination and the passengers alighted. Following directions along the long thin corridors that led out from the vessel, the atmosphere went from doomed to strangely excited as the group began to debate with one another what their new world would look like. They eventually reached a large circular opening: the entrance to their diorama. They stepped through one by one, guided by the Authorities.

Red looked up at the dimly-lit seacity before her. It was so much taller than she'd imagined. She felt even smaller and more alone as she looked around at the growing crowds.

One group of people in front of her seemed particularly distressed. Civilians were frenetically asking Authorities questions, but received little or no response. Red froze and felt a sharp tingle creep along her spine when she overheard an officer beside her:

"It looks as if the last ten groups are stuck, but we're sure it's momentary. We're being told it's a technical fault. They'll fix it within minutes."

What followed, was an epic sound louder than all of the world's volcanoes erupting simultaneously. The Shell rocked uncontrollably, swaying with the current of the ocean. Everyone from citizens to Authorities were knocked to their knees. Instantly, people everywhere were on the ground with a look of horror painted across their faces. Only the Authorities could mask their emotions with the dome-shaped helmets they donned.

Once again, Red felt the world slow down as she fell forward and hurtled towards the floor beneath her feet. The realisation that her mother was gone forever, along with the beautiful world above, hit her faster and harder than the cold metallic floor of The Shell. The fact that she never got the chance to say goodbye to her mother did not dawn on her until much later when she awoke in a room full of Authorities. Watching the footage of the world above filled with raining ash.

* * *

Delta breathed a sigh of relief as she stepped into the enormous greenhouse and found Red lying sideways on some soil. It may have been artificially grown, but being surrounded by so much greenery made Red feel peaceful. It reminded her of all the natural things she, like so many others, took for granted as a child.

Delta would often find her here. She would have to squeeze through tiny gaps in the greenhouse's wall and climb up a tall mound of soil to reach the green allotments that Red adored. This was completely illegal, but Delta knew it was not the time to lecture her friend.

"Look Red, I'm sorry. I–"

"Shhh…" Red interrupted her as she sat up and pointed her finger towards Delta's mouth. She smiled, then said:

"It doesn't matter. Come lay here and listen with me a while."

Delta stepped slowly over to where Red had been lying and got down on her side to join her friend.

Two old friends lay in silence with their ears pressed against the soil as they listened to the bionic throb of the Reactor beneath. There was something comforting about the hypnotic pulse. Like the sound of a mother's heartbeat to her baby in the womb.

The argument the girls had been having just a few hours prior felt like a distant memory, fading away into the night.

FOUR

Dozens of cameramen and other members of crew collided into one another as they readied themselves for Ivan Spencer's broadcast. His Personal Assistant, Han Eden, brought him his black coffee as makeup artists and stylists combed over his wispy white hair and powdered his pasty gaunt cheeks. Han could sense his boss' impatience mounting as he tapped his shoe against the side of his seat and drummed his fingers frantically upon his knee.

"Keep calm, president. Have you memorised all your lines?" Han fixed the electronic cue in front of Ivan ready for the televised statement.

"Of course I have, Han," Ivan Spencer replied. "I just detest having a camera in my face. You know that."

Han did know this. He'd been working for Ivan Spencer for enough years to know every last detail about him. How he liked to have his first coffee of the day before being briefed on any of his duties. How he would refuse to eat anything that wasn't macrobiotic and newly harvested. He knew that his mood could go from bouncy and joyous to erratic and vexed in less than a second. But above all, he knew that despite the fact that his leader spent so much of his life in front of the lens, he absolutely loathed being the subject of a camera.

Han slowly stepped backwards and gave a nod to the surrounding crew to go live in 5, 4, 3…

Red drew in a deep breath as she braced herself for what she was about to hear. She sat through every single one of the government's visual and audio broadcasts and every single time she would regret it. She could never understand why she seemed to be the only person capable of seeing through Ivan Spencer's transparent words. This broadcast would prove to be no exception.

"Good evening citizens of the United Underworld. It is with great pleasure that I address you tonight with some fantastic developments that we have been making on land. Firstly though, I would like to take this opportunity to address the silver lining of such an unfortunate situation we found ourselves in ten years ago this month.

"It is my belief that everything happens for a reason. This is often hard to believe when we look around at all of the crime and destruction that takes place in our world. A world that was created to protect our society from the Day of Judgment. All of the injustice that takes place in a world that was meant to bring us together in our darkest hour. Some may question God's actions altogether when He threw a ball of fire upon our planet and destroyed our land and took away our homes.

But it is important that we keep our faith and remember that everything the Lord decides to do is done to test us.

"It is this very reason that I come before you today to remind you all of the silver lining that paves the streets of our United Underworld beneath the oceans. Even the Apocalypse itself, as brutal and catastrophic as it was, did not prevent us from moving forward and becoming stronger as a nation. This is why we must respect each other and respect the seacity that has kept us safe while we repair our beloved land above."

Red rolled her eyes and poured herself a glass of wine that had a very similar shade to her hair.

I can say what I want about him, she thought, *but he's still the best liar around.* She swung back a large gulp of the drink as she listened to the president continue his speech.

"So tonight dear citizens, I come to you with both reassuring news about our developments over ground, and also an inspiring way of dealing with our current circumstance as we wait.

"Now, in regards to the advancements we have made over ground: I can inform you that we have come on by leaps and bounds since we last spoke. Although the toxic fumes in the air are still far too dangerous to allow citizens back onto land, we have managed to get at least seven different types of plants to begin to grow, meaning plantation developments are well underway. I truly believe that the first set of citizens could get back above the ocean as soon as the beginning of next year."

At this point, Red couldn't contain her frustration any longer. She threw her glass of wine over the three-dimensional hologram of Ivan Spencer's head in front of her. Aura leapt from her lap in shock and scurried out of the room.

"The beginning of next year?" She asked rhetorically out loud. "How much longer do we have to wait?" As the red liquid dripped onto the wafer-thin device projecting his speech, the visualisation of Ivan Spencer's head flickered and then went out completely. Before Red even had a chance to react, the sound of the door buzzer echoed throughout the room. She answered the door to be greeted by her new therapist once again.

"Oh, it's you." Red turned back around and headed towards the kitchen to grab a cloth. "I bet early next year seems really soon to you too doctor, doesn't it?"

Ethan let himself in and followed his patient into the living space where she was wiping what was left of her glass of wine from the projector pad.

"I take it you missed your mouth slightly?" Ethan smiled to himself as he walked over and tried to help.

"It's fine, I've got it," Red signalled at him to sit down as she finished the job herself. "Besides, I wouldn't be doing this if your precious president hadn't wound me up so much with his ridiculous speech."

Ethan sat down, scratched his shaven head and unlocked his pad before scrolling down the screen to find Red's empty file. "Oh dear, what has he done to upset you?"

Red switched the hologram back on to find Ivan Spencer continuing his speech about over ground developments.

"Early next year. That's when he thinks the first group of civilians will be able to go back above land. And he calls that a development?" She sat down next to her therapist and put her face into her hands. Her hair fell in front of her face like red curtains covering the stage of a theatre. "He's been saying that for the last decade. But it never happens."

"You hate him, don't you?" Ethan asked softly. Red looked up slowly and pushed her mane away from her eyes.

She poured herself a fresh glass of wine and pulled out a cigarette.

"Smoke, doctor?"

"No," he responded. "No thank you."

"I thought as much." Red lit her cigarette and inhaled deeply as if it was the last one she was ever going to have. "My father died when I was eight years old. He worked away from home a lot. I rarely saw him at all to be honest."

"I'm sorry," Ethan said genuinely.

"It's ok, I'm not looking for sympathy." Red inhaled more smoke from her cigarette before flicking ash into a crystal tray. "He worked for the government. I never knew what he did, or how he died. My mother never told me. The truth is I don't even know if she knew for certain. Either that or she was just trying to protect me from the truth."

Red stood up and walked towards the window where she looked out into the haunting darkness of The Shell.

"Either way I will never know. I lost my mother when the asteroid hit, she was in one of the groups that got stuck above the ground."

Red looked back at the handsome stranger in the room and narrowed her eyes. "No is the answer to your question, doctor, I don't hate him. But I don't trust him any more than I trust the motive behind your visits." Red sat back down and put out her cigarette. Her words were spoken with conviction as her expression changed from vulnerable to stern. It was as if she'd realised how much she'd let her guard down and opened up. Her hair fell back in front of her face as the theatre curtains fell shut once more.

"So I guess you're going to sit there and write everything I've just told you down, and take it back to the government? Maybe you could write a little summary about me to show them how much closer you think you've got to cracking me than the last one did. Maybe you could all study me like a statistic once you're done with pretending that you're interested in how I feel or what I think–"

"You've got me all wrong," Ethan interrupted Red before she could continue her attack. "You think I'm pretending to care about what you're saying just to feed back some stupid lies to the government? Get real Red, this is just a job. A job I'm lucky to have in our current situation."

Red looked to the floor as she realised how presumptuous she'd been. Or at least the small amount of effort she'd put into hiding her assumptions. At least what her therapist had said about having a job was true. There was nothing left of the economy. When word got out about the asteroid heading towards earth, everyone with stocks frantically tried to sell as share prices plummeted on the exchange. Even the wealthiest of businessmen found themselves jobless and soon in poverty as they headed beneath the ocean. It seemed that working for the government as a therapist made you one of the more fortunate in society.

"What you have got to understand Red," Ethan began, "and I mean this with all due respect, is that you are not the only person to have lost someone. You are certainly not the only one to lose someone through the asteroid's impact." Ethan turned towards the hologram of their leader who finished his speech before some hypnotic yet encouraging music began to play. "He's not a bad man. He's just trying to put things right and give humanity a second chance. He's trying to bring back light to a world sent into darkness."

Red stared at Ethan's blue eyes, as they seemed to glaze over staring at the screen. *Such a beautiful face,* she thought to herself. *Shame they've got to his mind too.*

The mesmerising music continued to play as the two young adults sat without words for what seemed like eternity. In another room, Aura purred quietly as she slept.

* * *

Some believe that destiny is written in the stars. That there's no such thing as coincidence. But Kyan Eisenberg had a very different outlook. Perhaps due to his career as a journalist in the Old World, he was used to using logic and facts to craft stories together that would sell.

But on the same night that Red and Ethan were glued to the holographic presentation of Ivan Spencer's speech, Kyan was on the opposite side of The Shell broadcasting the presentation in the United Underworld Studios. And although they didn't know it yet, all three of the young people's paths would soon become intertwined. Whether this was through fate or sheer chance.

With a mesmerising musical flourish, Kyan finalised the production with the words LOOK TO THE SKY AND KNOW

THAT YOUR LORD IS WATCHING OVER YOU AT ALL TIMES. He then walked through the studio towards his locker without saying a single word to the rest of his crew, before packing away his equipment.

There was nothing glamorous about the United Underworld Studio's building in the way someone might imagine. Instead, it looked more like a large unfinished warehouse. Rusty walls with paint peeling off them surrounded by dozens of dirty desks. But what the government had seemingly spent a lot of money on was the advanced technology used to communicate messages to the inhabitants of The Shell. Kyan packed his last pieces of equipment away into his backpack, threw on his grubby denim jacket and stepped out into the night.

Kyan's face had something worn about it. His dark skin was tired and covered with lines, but not from smiling. There were bags underneath his deep brown eyes and he kept a thin strip of his afro-textured hair running across the side of his otherwise shaved head, creating the style of a short mohawk.

As Kyan began to make his way home, he thought about how much he despised his job and longed for things to change. His work was a simple process of being sent film footage from the government that he would then broadcast to the public. He would watch the projection of Ivan Spencer sitting in his large chair in a secret studio making the same promises that he had been making for the last decade. Kyan felt powerless and frustrated that he was supporting this process. But what could he do? He was lucky to even have work in The Shell. Besides, everyone worked for the government in one way or another. And in his eyes, it beat being an engineer.

Before the asteroid hit, Kyan had worked as a feature writer for the online news outlet *The Daily Liberate*. Being somewhat of a radical journalist, the role had suited him perfectly. Out of all the digital dailies, *The Liberate* was the most renowned for its investigative journalism. This made it the perfect match for Kyan's strong thirst for justice. He contributed to the digital title for many years and probably would have worked right up to the world's final moments if he'd been able to. But once news got out about the asteroid, chaos broke out in the Old World and all businesses became outmoded immediately. Media outlets were terminated along with thousands of other huge corporations as Ivan Spencer prepared to have everybody transported to safety below.

Once underneath, it was as if Ivan Spencer had a blank canvas to work with as he developed a new system of employment. Many were left without any work at all, so when Kyan was selected to join the United Underworld's broadcasting team, there was no way that he could say no. It just happened that he disbelieved the intentions of the government entirely, making him feel like a hypocrite every time he broadcasted one of Ivan Spencer's announcements.

Kyan reached his level earlier than he thought he would. The traffic had been worse than usual all week and he had noticed a lot of boy podracers about. There had been more accidents than normal and just like the shortage of Authorities in The Shell, there was also a disturbing lack of paramedics. He found it unnerving how such a small amount of hospitals and surgeries had been developed in The Shell. As if Ivan Spencer hadn't wanted to spend money on such necessities.

Instead, there was a subversive black market of practitioners who worked autonomously to treat the sick citizens.

Kyan's flat looked just as dingy inside as it did on the outside. His elevator didn't work and there were cracks all along the walls and corridor of the level that allowed rats to come and go freely. The Shell was full of rats. They had inadvertently been brought down in freights that contained the grain and other resources to grow food. It was simply impossible to rid the United Underworld of all its faults and vermin. Most of The Shell's supplies were used to repair problems within the Reactor itself. Albeit an incredible design, in many ways the United Underworld was like a skeleton of a body that had never been given its flesh.

Kyan entered the code to his room and collapsed in a heap on his bed. After a short while, he shot up, filled a large cylinder with coffee and sat at his messy desk. Could it really be 21:00 already? The young man rubbed his eyes and unlocked his pad. Despite his fatigue, he would make sure he devoted at least an hour a day to the work he genuinely cared about. In his eyes, this was his duty as an honourable citizen. This was the least he could do.

Kyan opened up the administration homepage of Shareflow and logged in. *Shareflow* was a website the tech-savvy journalist used to leak any information about the government he managed to get his hands on. He'd launched the site after he discovered a flaw in the government's censorship barriers over the UUW and had been running it for a few months. He seized the opportunity to develop a site that allowed him to share information freely and expose hidden truths about Ivan

Spencer and his regime.

The Shareflow website had a simplistic design with minimal use of colour. The majority of the page would show up transparent on a computer pad screen or on a holographic projection, giving off the effect that the crisp text was floating in the air. This contrasted the government's bold, colourful and patriotic style.

As well as any information Kyan got his hands on, he would encourage his audience to contribute their own secret findings about the government. To do this, an anonymous email address could be found in the contact section of the site. That was the first place Kyan looked as he logged into the website's administration page, to be greeted by a new notification. Leaks would normally come in from anonymous senders, but this message clearly said that it was from a Professor Prothero. Intrigued, Kyan opened it.

"Whoa!" he moved backwards in shock as a blinding hologram of the scientist flickered to life inches away from Kyan's nose.

The old man's tired face lit up the room as a thin beam was released from below the computer pad's screen. The scientist had obviously been close to the sensor when he recorded his message, as the hologram displayed an enlarged and rather distorted three-dimensional projection of his head. Although flickering, it was clear enough to see the lines across the scientist's face and the details of his fine silver hair. Before Kyan had a chance to dim the hologram, Prothero began to speak.

"To whom it may concern. I have made a seriously important finding that I must share with you right away," the professor's tone was both stern and urgent. "I wish to meet with whomever is running this site to leak this breakthrough as soon as possible. It is crucial that we alert as many people as we can!" As the message finished and the hologram disappeared, Kyan found Professor Prothero's contact code, reached for his connector and frantically tapped the digits in.

By the time Kyan reached Professor Prothero's laboratory, he feared what he might find. He knew that the government was hot on the tail of whoever was behind Shareflow, as well as any other whistleblowers involved, making it all the more important for them to never leave a trace. He was also aware of what sort of fate would await them if discovered. Particularly for himself, given his job title. It was surprising that the government had not yet found a way to shut the site down, but Kyan's technological skills far outweighed the work of Ivan Spencer's web teams.

After ringing the buzzer several times to no avail, Kyan tried calling the scientist only to be met with a disconnected line. Growing frustrated, the secret activist knew he would have to break the door down. Disguised in the uniform of an Authority, something he'd managed to easily acquire through his workplace where all sorts of government attire was kept, Kyan aimed his small yet lethal raygun at the door's electronic lock. He shot the weapon, destroying the mechanism and unlocking the door. Wires sizzling, he forced the buckled door open. He then grasped his weapon tightly as he turned the hallway that led into Prothero's laboratory.

Just as he feared. The scientist, along with all of his equipment, was nowhere to be seen.

FIVE

When Red approached her bookstore the following day, the first thing she noticed was an unusual smell. The ashy scent lingered around the corner as she picked up the pace. Her thoughts were becoming scattered and erratic. Her vision blurred.

As she turned around the corner, Red's worst nightmare had been brought to life. An enormous cloud of dust and debris surrounded what had once been her beloved bookstore. All that remained were the building's bones, a skeleton with thousands of shredded pages floating in the air. Her throat turned dry as sand. Her rapidly-beating heart dropped to her gut.

"No!" she screamed as she sprinted towards the demolished building, attempting to run inside. A hand grabbed her arm.

"Don't go in there dear, it's dangerous!" Marcus' warm and familiar voice stopped Red in her tracks as she looked on at her treasured shop in dismay. The spine of an old hardback book lay by her boot, so cindered she was unable to make out the title. A large shard of glass from one of the building's windows had pierced through the burnt strip of fabric. Red spun around and stared at her old friend who shared her stunned look.

"Marcus, what… what happened?" Red's eyes darted from side to side as she attempted to stay focused.

"I only got here a few minutes before you. I had the fright of my life worrying that you might be in there," Marcus spoke slowly as he struggled to find the words he wanted to say. "Probably just a group of bored vandals. Then again, you know me. I wouldn't put this past the Authorities for a single second. I am so, so sorry my dear."

Marcus clutched Red's hands between his and offered her a sympathetic look, but he could barely disguise his own sadness. Red shook her head then sat down on the cracked pavement next to her destroyed bookstore.

He's right, she thought. *I wouldn't put it past the Authorities either. In fact, I'm certain this was their doing. If not with their own sly hands, then through forcing those of supposed 'vandals'.* Red shook her head as if to escape her own mind. She turned again to her elderly friend.

"What I can't understand, Marcus, perhaps even more than the fact that this has happened, is why I feel nothing." She turned to face him again to reveal not even a single tear in her eyes. "I'm completely numb. But it's not even from the shock. I just feel… nothing." Red turned away again and stared at the dirty ground beneath her feet.

Marcus slowly and delicately sat down beside his friend as his expression turned fearful. He wrapped his bony arm around her and began to speak clear words in a precise tone:

"My dear. Whatever happens in this life, no matter how awful or undeserved, no matter what trials and tribulations you are put through or the countless ways in which you will be tried and tested: never let them harden you enough to feel nothing. Always remember the fire that is in your heart, dear, and use your anger. Use your passion and use your love to push yourself further and bring you closer to achieving your dreams."

The pair then sat silently on the ground in front of the graveyard of literature that had once been the shop they'd loved so intensely. Red wished more than anything that she would be able to cry, but nothing came. All she could feel was a startling sense of vacancy.

On her way home, Red's mind was in a thousand different places but she couldn't focus on a single thought. A kaleidoscope of suppositions drifted through her head as she walked the full three and a half miles home along the artificially-lit streets. *Maybe it wasn't the Authorities,* she wondered to herself. *Maybe it was just kids, like Marcus said. Let's face it. I probably would've done the same.*

Vandalism existed everywhere you looked in The Shell. There was violence on almost every street corner and you could smell the scent of fear in the air. Older children and teenagers were the worst. Initially, the idea of moving under the ocean had seemed exciting to them, but this soon wore off once they realised they would not be returning to daylight anytime soon. Generally, young people could get their hands on a piece of electronic weaponry fairly easily, not realising how lethal the technology could be. Shareflow had reported cases of children as young as six and seven using rayguns to seriously injure – and even kill – Authorities. Those children were never seen or heard of again.

Red slowly turned down the narrow alleyway that led to her street. As she passed the twisted, wilting fencing that resembled bionic vegetation, her expression remained glazed. She stuffed her hand into the pocket of her studded leather jacket to retrieve her sixth cigarette since leaving the shop. She paused as she noticed a shadowy figure standing outside the entrance to her level. The stranger began to move out of the darkness towards her. She instantly recognised Ethan as his striking face hit the light.

As the therapist got closer to her, Red realised he was holding a large bunch of yellow roses in his hands. How had he known they were her favourite? She rolled her eyes as it dawned on her. Delta. She must have given Ethan this information in a way of making up for what she'd said during her argument with Red. There had been no hard feelings as far as Red was concerned. They were too good friends for that, practically sisters. And just like real sisters, the very next morning they had both acted like nothing had happened the night before. But this was typical Delta behaviour to think that a guy would be the solution to a problem. *Unless it had been his idea,* Red wondered to herself, half smiling.

Ethan greeted his patient with a sympathetic expression on his face as he passed the flowers to her.

"I came to meet you from work. So I saw what happened," Ethan chose his words carefully. "I got straight into my pod to head over. I'm so sorry, Red."

Red glanced at the flowers and then continued towards the front door of her level without taking them from him.

"You're not going to win me over with flowers, doctor." Without looking back, she proceeded towards the rusty elevator inside.

Ethan followed closely behind, still clutching onto the roses. "Oh well. It was worth a try, I guess."

Inside, Red threw her jacket onto the sofa and swiftly moved towards the kitchen. She fetched a bottle of red wine and a single glass as if it was second nature.

"Do you stock anything else in this kitchen?" Ethan asked, helping himself to a vase to put the roses in.

Aura crept out from behind the sofa where she'd been sleeping and purred loudly.

"Not really, doctor. Nor do I have any intention to." Red sat down, scooped her feline friend up into her arms and gave her a tight squeeze. "I just can't believe how much misfortune I endure sometimes. It was like I was born cursed or something."

Ethan sat down beside his troubled patient and attempted to make eye contact. Red eventually turned to look at him. She'd never noticed what an extraordinary shade of blue his eyes were, like two planet Earths if all the land was submerged. She also hadn't noticed the golden hue to his complexion. His radiant skin juxtaposed Red's bone-white flesh that seemed to grow paler as each day passed.

"Hey listen, why don't we go out for a drink somewhere instead?" Ethan asked with a sudden burst of enthusiasm. "We could both do with a change of scenery. Of course it would be totally against regulations—"

"I'm in," Red interrupted with a mischievous grin that broke across her face.

Within minutes, the pair were racing across the corroded yet intricate rails of The Shell in Ethan's pod. Red peered outside of the robust, blacked-out glass that all pods had built into their sides. They were heading in a direction that was completely alien to her. In spite of the fact that the United Underworld was a dangerous place, the southeast section had a reputation of being a civilised area. This zone, the Docklands, was where the enormous vessels that had once been used to move civilians down to The Shell were stationed.

These same vessels were used to transport select government officials to an enormous station above the ground that had been built exclusively for Ivan Spencer and his regime. This base was also rumoured to hold the construction workers who'd begun operations outside of The Shell. Footage shown sometimes in televised transmissions displayed these workers wearing oxygen masks to develop the *New Overworld*.

Red leaned on her arm as her eyes darted rapidly side-to-side, trying to adjust to this vaguely-familiar area. The area she first saw as she arrived in The Shell. She began to notice far more Authorities monitoring the section and far fewer vandalised buildings. She pushed her thick hair out of her eyes and turned to look at Ethan. He looked back at her with a slightly concerned expression.

"We shouldn't go too far into the Docklands, Red," he said sternly. "This is government-only territory." Before she had time to reply, Ethan had sat up and flicked a few switches on the pod's control panel. It came to a sudden halt and opened up, allowing the two to climb out.

"I know a good bar just two blocks away from here," Ethan said. "We can walk it."

When Ethan had suggested going out for a drink, Red had imagined somewhere rowdy with loud music. Somewhere she could lose herself on a dance floor. But the bar they arrived at was quite the opposite, with very few people inside and a jukebox in the corner. She walked straight over to it and started to scroll through the songs on its screen.

"So this is your idea of a good time?" she teased, trying to decide on a song to select.

"Sure, it's quiet. But it serves good whisky," Ethan said walking over to the bar. "Do you drink whisky?"

Red made a grimace as her bitten-down fingernail tapped on the jukebox's dusty screen. "Red wine will do just fine."

As Ethan headed to the bar and immediately immersed himself in a hearty conversation with the old barman, Red continued to swipe her finger through the tracks on the jukebox. While she moved through each genre, she turned her attention to Ethan out of the corner of her eye. He really did have a charm. What was it about him that managed to light up the entire room when he walked in? Red felt herself cringing at her own thoughts as she turned her focus back to the jukebox. She didn't do crushes, particularly with someone who worked for the government. That would go against every single thing she believed in, all at once.

Unable to make up her mind, Red finally selected an electronic punk song, which she turned up to maximum volume before sitting down. Frantic noise came blasting out of the jukebox, much to the dismay of the few other people that sat in the once-quiet bar.

"You're going to get us kicked out," Ethan exclaimed before taking a large sip of his drink. "Don't you ever stop trying to rile people up?"

"Not really. Even if I didn't try I'd probably still annoy them." Red smiled as she picked up the glass her therapist had brought to her.

"So you take wine off me, but not flowers. At least I know for next time, I guess." Ethan smiled as he drank some more of his whisky.

"Next time?" Red looked confused. "I'm sorry, doctor. But this is not going to be a regular thing. I'm not really sure why I'm here now."

Ethan looked genuinely hurt. "I don't understand why you're so defensive all the time, Red. I know you're young–" Ethan stopped himself, immediately as he realised the backlash to follow.

"Don't patronise me, doctor," she shouted. "You're supposed to be a therapist." Red downed the rest of her wine and looked away.

Ethan continued, "That doesn't mean I think you're naive, Red. I'm fully aware of the darkness you've witnessed in your life." Ethan must have been at least six years older than his patient, albeit hard to tell. You could sense that he had experienced life, mostly in the way he spoke, but he still had a youthfulness about him. An innocence. It was as if he'd been completely unaffected by his own misfortunes.

"So come on then, doctor. What's your story?" Red met

Ethan's focus once more, as if trying to unravel knots hidden deep within his eyes. Sometimes she felt that despite her efforts to come across enigmatic and ambiguous, she could be as transparent as a windowpane. Ethan on the other hand had a genuine air of mystery about him that she couldn't help but feel captivated by. "You already know mine."

There was a brief pause before Ethan spoke.

"Leyla. That's the name of my younger sister," the therapist's eyes glazed over as he spoke in a way that made the hairs stand up on the back of Red's neck. "She got left behind too, when we were moved under. She was one of the people who didn't make it down. Just like your mother."

Red's stare went from a look of confusion and fear to that of empathy. For the first time ever with the therapist, Red felt her guard come down as she reached her hand to his and gave it a soft squeeze.

"Then you know the answer to your questions, doctor. You know then because you feel what I feel," she said delicately. "Next time you want to know where the anger comes from. You should know that it just comes."

There was then silence for at least a minute or two. Finally, after what felt to Red like eternity, he agreed: "It just comes."

Then they kissed.

In a moment that seemed completely disconnected from time, electricity flowed through the pair as their lips connected. Red felt every cell that made up her body tingle and bounce. The dark cloud above her head moved aside and for the first time, for as long as she could remember, she felt light radiate through her. True happiness, in every sense of the word.

But as soon as it dawned on Red what was happening, she quickly pulled away.

"I should go." She turned and began to walk in the opposite direction from where Ethan was standing.

"Red, wait. Let me drop you home…"

But it was too late. She'd already disappeared into the night.

SIX

As the artificial dawn arrived, Kyan left his level for work. A whole day had passed since he visited Professor Prothero's laboratory only to be met with an empty room and a disconnected line when he tried calling. He knew that whatever this man had uncovered, the government had caught on and prevented him from sharing this knowledge.

As Kyan climbed into his pod to head to work, he winced at the thought of what could have happened to him. *Surely he would be dead by now.* Or worse, he might have been kept alive. Perhaps the Authorities had thrown the man over ground where he would have choked on the toxic fumes, or burnt to death in the flames still raging across what was left of the land.

It's not worth thinking about, Kyan thought to himself. But what he was really concerned about, was that he could be missing vital information. Information that would have proven to people across The Shell exactly what he had been fighting for so long to uncover.

The trouble was, even Kyan had reached the point where he doubted himself at times. Despite the scraps he uncovered from whispers across the newsroom or the odd anonymous person who sent him some information, Shareflow's humble readership generally did not seem to accept what they were reading. Everything he had uncovered was met with an initial shocked response, before his readers accepted or brushed off the information. If he uncovered something important, something big, something that affected everybody, would the public just ignore it?

But the burning desire Kyan held in his heart for truth and justice was enough to waive off any of these doubtful thoughts. It was as if this innate suspicion was the only thing that kept him from wanting to give in and remain silent. For as long as he would be able, Kyan had vowed not to remain silent. He was sure that he would be discovered sooner or later, particularly working so closely to the government, but he was prepared to dedicate the rest of whatever time he had left in his life to exposing exactly what was going on behind closed doors. If not to save himself, then to save future generations and their chance to rebuild what had once been a beautiful planet.

Kyan stopped his pod as he arrived at work. He stared up at the tall, clinical building that housed the United Underworld Studios and shuddered. He reluctantly got out of the pod and slowly paced towards the entrance. *Another day in paradise.*

* * *

Red was already awake and out of bed when Delta walked into the living room. She'd polished off a bowl of grain and oats and was sipping on a large metallic cylinder of black coffee. It was difficult for Red to get many vitamins from her food, as fruit and vegetables were scarce in The Shell and she hated the idea of them being grown artificially.

Red also struggled with her protein intake seeing as she refused to eat insects. Insects were the cheapest and most accessible food available in The Shell, as so many had been brought down when the asteroid hit. But the idea of eating them had always disgusted her. Even before society had been transported to The Shell, red and white meat had become much rarer as there wasn't enough space to farm animals. Meat had become reserved only for the very wealthy.

Fish and other seafood, although expensive, were still available in the Old World. But once in The Shell, the government assured people that it would be too dangerous to eat any sea creatures that hadn't been killed by the asteroid's fumes, as they could be toxic. Whatever the case, Red refused to eat insects entirely so she lived on a very minimal and dull diet of grains and supplementary pills. But to her, this felt like the least of her problems.

Red sat scrolling through Shareflow for any updates but there hadn't been any for days. The last one said how delays had been made with progress over ground again as Ivan Spencer had been spending too much time with his daughter, Carmen.

Carmen was an only child and it was never really determined who her mother was. Ivan Spencer had certainly never been *seen* with a woman over the years and no one ever dared to ask the question. A slim girl with sallow skin and a gaunt face similar to her father's, Carmen changed the colour of her blunt, bobbed hair more times than the men who worked for the government shaved theirs.

Carmen was rarely seen in public and it was never known exactly what she did. Red found it doubtful that she had to work at all, but always found her lack of presence peculiar. It was also no real surprise that Carmen had slowed progress down through spending more time with her father, as the pair were notoriously close. But this was hardly regarded as a negative thing by society. The family bond warmed people, because family values were generally a thing of the past in The Shell.

Red, on the other hand, wasn't so warmed. It made her feel physically sick.

"I wasn't sure whether you'd be up yet," Delta said walking past her flatmate and towards the kitchen to make coffee. "Xave left early this morning so I'm running a bit late."

Red kept her eyes glued to the pad as she zoomed in to take a closer look at the photograph of Carmen. Her hair was dyed green in this particular picture and she was wearing a short, metallic dress and fishnet tights. *Well, she has good style at least*, Red thought to herself sniggering. *Shame about her blood.*

"Red?" Delta interrupted her friend's thoughts.

"Oh yeah, sorry," Red finally replied. "I couldn't sleep. I had another one of those weird dreams."

"About your mother?" Delta asked with a concerned tone. She sipped her coffee and passed another cup to Red.

"Thanks. Yeah, the exact same one," Red said slowly. "You

know, I know it sounds crazy. But it's like she's... reaching out to me or something."

"Reaching out to you? You mean, reaching out to you from another life?" Delta asked as she tried to hide her confusion.

"Yeah, maybe. Perhaps." Red always chose her words carefully when speaking with Delta about religion. While Red was open-minded to alternative viewpoints, she ultimately considered herself an atheist. Delta on the other hand, like most of the inhabitants of The Shell, very much believed in God. It was as if they had to. Like they needed a crutch to lean on. Hope that there was still a Heaven out there waiting for them beyond the dark and dreariness of the United Underworld.

Ivan Spencer, just like his father before him, was a very strict Catholic and encouraged society to share his views. Religion in general had become a notion of the past in the latter half of the twenty-first century, but this had all changed once the Spencer regime arrived. By the time Ivan Spencer moved society down to The Shell, he ensured that every household had a Bible to help guide them through their hardships. And every speech he made referenced *the Lord* somewhere. This was the main reason Red rejected the idea of God.

She was also a realist and found it hard to believe there was somebody or something out there watching over her and the world she loved. After all, where had God been when the asteroid hit the earth and destroyed her mother along with everything else He had supposedly created?

"Or perhaps reaching out to me from this life," Red added quietly under her breath.

Delta turned and looked at her friend with concern.

From time to time Red had mentioned how she still believed that her mother was alive somewhere, even though she herself knew that this was simply denial. She knew there was no way her mother, or any other human who had been left behind above the ground, could have survived the asteroid's blow and the meteoroids it created.

"Red, listen. An awful thing happened yesterday and I know it's going to take a lot of time to… move on from it," Delta spoke softly yet firmly. "But at some stage you will need to decide what you're going to do for money now instead. Why don't you consider coming to work alongside Xave and I at the Reactor? It's not so bad. In fact, we have a lot of laughs in between. It pays enough. And you and I are lucky enough to keep our hair!"

The sharp glare Red shot towards her friend said everything she needed to say without even opening her mouth. It wasn't the first time Delta had made the suggestion which she considered ridiculous, but this time she decided not to dignify it with a verbal response.

Delta finished the last drop of coffee from her cup, rubbed the side of Red's arm gently and smiled.

"All right, all right. It was just a suggestion." She stood up and walked towards the door. "Try to get some air, Red. You don't want to be stuck on that thing all day." Delta pointed towards the pad, before leaving the flat.

"If only I *could* get some air," Red said to herself sarcastically. As if in reply, Aura meowed loudly while creeping out quietly from Red's bedroom.

"Morning, sweetheart. I guess you want to be fed, don't you?" Red smiled at her tiny feline friend and stroked her all the way across her shiny black back. "Give me ten minutes, I just need to do something quickly."

Although she had no intention of doing what Delta had suggested and work alongside her at the Reactor, she did have a plan as to what she could do next for work. And it didn't matter to her at all how well it paid.

Red scrolled down the Shareflow page on her pad and tapped the contact button. A thin red beam projected out from underneath the pad's screen ready to record the young girl's message. As she spoke, Red wondered why she hadn't tried this sooner.

"To whoever it is that is in charge of this brave and brilliant website. Please listen to what I have to say," Red spoke clearly and with conviction as Aura scuttled away into the kitchen. "I think what you are doing is incredible. I don't know who you are, but I share the same fears and beliefs as you. I would like to meet you as soon as possible, to discuss how I can help you with your selfless and extremely necessary mission in uncovering the government's lies."

Red moved closer towards the narrow red beam as she read out her address.

"Please, whoever you are… let me join you. We cannot fight this battle on our own."

After she finished her heartfelt message, Red went from tenacious to tender as she headed to the kitchen to feed her once-stray cat. On her way, she picked up the dusty old book she'd borrowed from Marcus and put it in her bag to return to him. She didn't expect to feel like reading it anytime soon. She had bigger things on her mind.

As Red made her way towards the door, her connector started to hum. It was Ethan, again. This was the fourth time he had tried calling since she left him at the bar the night before. She'd decided a bit of space was needed, particularly as she couldn't deny the growing feelings she had towards him.

As much as she was beginning to care about Ethan, she still didn't trust him. How could she? It was too risky to become attached to someone who worked so closely with the government. Particularly someone who was being paid to observe her thoughts. Besides, Red was not the kind of girl to give her heart away to some guy she'd only just met. The truth was, she'd never given her heart away to anyone. Any relationship she'd experienced with the opposite sex over the years had been purely physical, ensuring she was the one who was firmly in control. If anything, Red had been the heartbreaker in all of her previous romantic endeavours.

So it was no surprise really that Red had decided not to mention what had happened the previous night to Delta. She knew she would have never lived it down. Her flatmate would have squealed with delight and the whole thing would have been extremely blown out of proportion. Instead, Red decided to find her own way home that night and attempt to forget the whole thing had even happened. Once she got over her embarrassment she would speak to Ethan, ensure her secret was safe with him and make sure he never visited again. Surely he would oblige if he really did have any feelings for her. Red was certain he didn't. It had to be some sort of malicious trick to try and get her to open up. It wasn't working.

Red set her connector to silent and left her flat.

SEVEN

Professor Prothero opened his eyes slowly and tried to make out where he was. He'd been conscious for a few minutes, but still hadn't found the strength to raise his eyelids. He was frightened what he might see if he did.

It was pitch black and all he could hear was a faint dripping sound somewhere in the distance. His arms were tied together above his head and the blood was completely drained, leaving them painfully numb. He couldn't feel his feet. The air was freezing cold against his bare skin, which ached and felt bruised. The air smelt damp and stagnant, a smell that brought back memories of entering The Shell for the first time. But stronger.

Just as the scientist's eyes began to adjust to the darkness, a masked figure stepped towards him with an excruciatingly bright torch in one hand, and what the professor could make out as a long tube in the other. As Professor Prothero attempted to open his mouth to shout, he realised that it was tightly taped shut. The stranger tore the tape from the scientist's mouth, lifted up what turned out to be a long weapon and then sent it crashing down on his head.

Blood burst out from the old man's mouth as he lost his consciousness once more.

* * *

Red stepped towards Marcus' door, clutching the dusty old book he'd lent her. She knew he would probably just tell her to hold on to it for as long as she wanted. It would be far more important to him that she found the time to read it than him needing it back.

But the truth was, for once Red didn't feel like reading. She also knew that she wouldn't be changing her mind anytime soon, as she had decided it was nearly the right time to finally escape the United Underworld.

She'd had a yearning to escape The Shell for as long as she could remember and she knew that the time was almost right. She could feel it in her weary bones. Reaching out to Shareflow was the initial stage of her plan, but she'd decided that if it came down to it: she would go alone.

There had been much speculation about the people who had tried to escape the United Underworld previously, even if nothing was officially confirmed. There had been talk about two young men who had devised an elaborate plan and even managed to get through the exit dressed as Authorities. But rumour had it that once they made it out into the ocean, they had both drowned trying to swim to the surface. Others believed they made it, but choked on the fumes once they reached the air.

There were other stories too, although Red was certain most of them were invented by the government. Told to scare people and turn them against the idea of ever trying to escape themselves. But it would take a lot more than that to change Red's mind. She would risk it all for the chance of seeing the world above again, no matter its current state.

Red knew how precious Marcus' books were to him. She understood this because she felt the exact same way. She didn't want to hang on to any of his treasured antiques any longer than she needed to. Particularly after her bookstore had been destroyed.

Marcus lived south of the River Tamesis. The canal ran through the centre of the United Underworld and was named after the original Latin word for London's equally murky River Thames in the Old World. It seemed far more apt in The Shell, seeing as the word 'Tamesis' was thought by linguists to mean dark. This was a fair distance from where Red resided. She'd always lived in the north.

To Red's surprise, a middle-aged woman answered the door. Her heart dropped as soon as she realised that the woman was a paramedic.

"What's happened? Where is he?" Red asked as she pushed past the woman and headed inside.

"Excuse me miss, you can't come in here. He—"

Red ignored the woman's words and stormed into Marcus' bedroom where she found him in bed, shivering. "Marcus?" Red walked over to her elderly friend. "What's happened?"

"Red! I'm so happy you're—" the old man's words were interrupted by his raspy cough. "I'm so happy that you're here, my dear."

The woman who had greeted Red at the door entered the room quietly, but Marcus signalled for her to leave.

"This is my friend, please give us a moment to speak," he said to the paramedic bluntly. The woman left the room without saying a word.

Marcus turned his attention back to his passionate friend before once again erupting into a chesty coughing fit. His face had turned a dull grey colour and his skin seemed to sag even more than normal on his thin face.

"What... happened?" Red asked slowly. "I know your cough has been getting worse, but I didn't realise—"

"Didn't realise what, my dear?" Marcus interrupted softly. "Didn't realise that I'm dying?"

Red turned her head away to communicate that she wasn't listening.

"Come on dear, you're a clever girl. Surely you've realised that I haven't got long left in me? It's not a place for an old man like me down here, with no fresh air or clean water."

Red turned back around to her friend and realised that she was fighting back tears. It was unlike her.

"I'm as good as dead to them now, anyway," Marcus continued, muttering under his breath. "They're finishing us old ones off first. But don't let them get to you…" Marcus held his hand up to hold Red's.

She couldn't hold back any longer. Her eyes welled up with tears as she tightly grasped onto her old friend's bony hand.

"Remember, my dear. Never give up. Never stop fighting." The old man began coughing again, the hoarseness even worse this time. "I'm just so glad you came, dear. I'm so glad I got to say goodbye."

Red looked on in dismay. "Stop it, stop it!" she screamed. "This is not goodbye, you're not going anywhere! We're going to get through this together."

Huge salty tears poured down her cheeks, a sensation she hadn't experienced in a very long time. "In fact," Red whispered to Marcus, "this is what I came to tell you. You know all those times I spoke about trying to escape? Well, I'm really going to do it this time. I'm going to get out and then I'm going to come back for you. I just need you to hang on. I need you to stay strong for me, and—"

Red froze. She realised that Marcus had already spoken his final words. Barely a minute or so later, his hand dropped out of her grasp and fell to the mattress beneath him. He let out a haunting rattling sound as he passed away.

"Marcus! Marcus, no!" Red shrieked as she realised that her friend's soul had already left his body. Like a balloon drifting off into the night's sky.

By the time the paramedic came back into the room, Red was already gone. The mousy-haired woman turned to look at the open window beside Marcus' bed where the curtains lay motionless, no wind to blow them and make them dance. She then looked back at the old man, lying as still as the green curtains. With a curl of red hair left lying upon his chest.

Ethan had only just turned away from the front door of

Red's flat after ringing the buzzer continuously to no avail when he felt his connector begin to hum. He reached for it in the pocket of his slate grey uniform jacket and was surprised to be met by Red's caller ID.

"Red, hi! How's it going?" Ethan asked in the friendliest tone he could manage.

"It's bad, Ethan," Red replied, clearly crying. "It's really, really bad."

Ethan's eyes opened in shock as he started to pace around the outside of Red's home in circles. Not only was he surprised to hear Red show vulnerability in her voice for the first time, but also to hear her call him by his actual name. Until this point, he'd been *doctor*. "Really, Red? What's happened? Where are you?"

"I need you right now," Red continued through her tears. "I need you, Ethan."

* * *

"I would like to meet you as soon as possible, to discuss how I can help you with your selfless and extremely necessary mission in uncovering the government's lies." The young redheaded woman's words echoed with conviction throughout Kyan's bedroom.

The recorded message came to an end and the hologram of her head flickered a few times before it disappeared into thin air. Kyan sat gazing at the exact same spot where the projection had been hovering, lighting up the entire room. He was deep in thought, mesmerised by what he'd just heard.

For the last six months that he had been running Shareflow, most of what he'd received was negative feedback, threats, abuse and requests for the website to be taken down. He understood that the government would be doing everything in its power to try and remove the whistleblowing platform, but he felt disappointed with society for not even attempting to process what he had to say.

There had been others who leaked information to him. There were more radicals living under the radar in the United Underworld, but they would never have given up their identity or asked to join Kyan with his mission. They knew that they would not only be risking their own lives, but the lives of their loved ones too.

The fact that Kyan had received a positive piece of feedback about his potentially-revolutionary creation was incredible enough. But the opportunity to have an ally in his radical endeavours was mind-blowing to the young rebel.

There were so many thoughts running through Kyan's head at this moment, such as the potential consequences of responding to a message like this. The first being the obvious: there was a very large possibility that the government was using this beautiful, redheaded woman to lure the person behind Shareflow into its clutches.

She'd left her name, address and connector number, which was displayed in a small information box on Kyan's screen. There was no doubt that if Kyan was going to visit the address that Red had provided, he would have to be masked and armed again. Just like when he paid Professor Prothero's laboratory a visit.

But it was still risky. He was only one man and if he arrived to a flat filled with Authorities, there wouldn't be a lot of hope left for him. Particularly given who he was and how closely he was linked to the government. Ivan Spencer would not tolerate that level of betrayal and humiliation.

On the other hand, it appeared that Professor Prothero had really existed. And if Kyan's suspicions were accurate, whatever the old scientist had wanted to leak could have quite possibly cost him his life. Could he really stand by and let the same thing happen to this young woman who shared his thirst for justice?

Kyan shuddered at the thought of an innocent person ending up in the hands of the government, before saving Red's address to his connector.

In the exact same moment that Kyan was debating whether to pay the mysterious stranger a visit, Red had ended up in the hands of the government. Albeit those hands belonging to a very handsome young therapist who she'd happened to develop strong feelings for.

Or had she? Perhaps Red just needed someone tonight. Could she really trust Ethan? This was a question Red still couldn't answer entirely, but on this particular night she needed a shoulder to cry on. She'd just lost one of the most important people in her entire world and she was certain that Ethan was a person that would listen and at least pretend to care. Wasn't that his job?

Ethan had held Red for almost three hours, wiping away all her tears. This truly was a first for her. She allowed her walls to come crumbling down just like the treasured bookstore she'd lost.

She cried for her father, gone before she got to know him. She cried for her mother, lost in an accident that should have been prevented. She cried for her dead friend, Marcus, who meant everything to her. She cried for her beautiful world, destroyed by a ruthless asteroid before being left abandoned. Finally, she cried for the people of The Shell. Duped into believing the words of a corrupt government.

Red smoothed her hand over Ethan's shaved head, gazed into his piercing blue eyes and leaned in to kiss him, passionately.

Ethan had been patient, waiting for the headstrong girl to kiss him on her own terms. He knew how important it was for her to be in control.

As Red's lips connected with the ones belonging to her therapist she noticed a tiny freckle on the side of his cheek. Like a single star lost in space. Before long, Red's tears had been replaced with pure lust as the pair began to tear each other's clothes off. A pile of slate grey fabric lay intertwined with distressed leather on the floor. Red's platform boots also slung to the ground.

Her connector began to buzz amidst the passion, but she switched it off and threw it towards the heap of clothes. If she had taken a moment to answer her connector, the owner of Shareflow would have greeted her.

As Red and Ethan were losing themselves in a whirlwind of intense attraction and emotion, Kyan was trying to get through to who he hoped would be an authentic ally. After trying a few more times he decided to grab his mask and raygun before making his way towards the young girl's address. He would have to move fast, if he wasn't already too late.

Despite Red not answering the phone to Kyan, she'd already decided what her next move was going to be. And there was no going back now.

EIGHT

Ethan opened his eyes and it dawned on him instantly that he was alone.

"Red?" he called out into the hallway, also realising that he was still naked.

"I'm making coffee," Red called out in a warm tone that Ethan had never heard her use before. "Give me two seconds."

He smiled to himself, laid back down and closed his eyes. What was this? A vexed young woman fighting the machine one minute, a domestic goddess the next? Perhaps he could get used to this new side of her.

Red slowly walked back into the room carrying two cylinders filled with black coffee. She was in her underwear. A mix-matched turquoise and neon yellow set that vividly contrasted her ivory skin and red hair. Ethan broke into a smile again as he thought back to the intimate night they had just shared.

"Thank you, Red." He sat up once more and held the hot

cylinder in his hands. "Look, about last night. I know you must think it was so unprofessional and—"

"Stop, it's okay Ethan," Red interrupted. "You don't have to explain anything. I enjoyed it." This time it was Red who was smiling.

Ethan's expression went from empathetic to relieved. "Great. I mean good… I'm glad," he explained, sipping the hot coffee carefully.

Red sat beside him on the bed as he began to play with her auburn locks with his other hand. Her hypnotic green eyes stared back at his as if searching for something.

"I want to thank you, Ethan. For coming to my rescue yesterday," Red said genuinely. "I know I have a lot of… walls around me. But I needed someone last night. I'm glad that someone was you."

Ethan smiled, this time taking a large gulp of coffee.

"You don't need rescuing, Red. And you know that," Ethan said, choosing his words carefully but honestly. "But we all need someone sometimes. And there's nothing wrong with that. I'm just glad you decided that person should be me."

Mere moments after he finished his sentence, Ethan's eyes dropped shut once more as he dropped his cup to the floor, spilling what coffee was left.

This is it, Red thought to herself, *there's no turning back now.* Her mind raced on overdrive, but she knew she had to compose herself and attempt to slow it down. What she was about to do was not only going to risk her own life, but potentially Ethan's too. She had to remind herself it was for the greater good, for everyone. For humanity.

Red took a deep breath, before pulling her unconscious therapist upright. She checked his breathing, ensuring it was regular, then grabbed a strong reel of tape and rope from the side pocket of her rucksack. After pulling his underwear back on to protect his modesty, Red wrapped tape around Ethan's mouth before finally tying his arms and legs together with the rope.

It's not that Red didn't have genuine feelings for her therapist. In some ways, this was part of the problem. She couldn't have let herself become too close to someone who worked for the government, particularly someone who was so blinded by its lies. She was certain that Marcus' death was connected to the living conditions designed by Ivan Spencer and his regime. She knew she had to do something. She couldn't just let her friend die in vain.

Red had made sure that she only poured enough chemical into Ethan's drink to knock him out and keep him unconscious for just as long as necessary. Her aim was not to kill him, or anybody for that matter. She simply needed to get outside and finally get some answers. She needed to visit the Overworld. And to do this, she would need to be disguised. She would need to be a man.

Red reached for her rucksack again, this time to pull out a small laser shaver. Without another thought the young woman began to remove her long ruby locks, sending them floating to the ground beneath her. The same determined look remained on her face the entire time she shaved away a symbol of her femininity and innocence. Of a once young girl, afraid of all the things going on around her. Afraid of what she'd lost and the thought of losing even more. She removed her entire head of hair, making room for a shaved scalp that closely mirrored the one belonging to Ethan.

As if possessed, Red threw the shaver to the ground where it landed directly on her bed of red hair. Her heart pounded rapidly in her chest, like a hammer repeatedly hitting a steel drum. She then pulled on Ethan's slate grey therapist uniform, before searching his entire flat for weapons. All she could find was a taser, which alongside her switchblade would have to suffice until she managed to get hold of a raygun.

Red lifted the unconscious therapist upright and began to drag him towards the bathroom where she planned to lock him in. She had no plans to leave Ethan for dead. She knew it would be a matter of time before he was found. She just needed a head start to escape. And she needed his identity.

"I'm sorry, Ethan. Really I am," she explained rhetorically. "I will be back for you. This is just something I need to do. And I can't let you stop me."

With that, Red locked the bathroom door and set a new passcode for it. She then left his flat and jumped into his pod. It was time.

* * *

Delta rolled her eyes as she heard the humming sound of her front door. This was the third day in a row she'd missed a ride with Xavier to work, so she didn't want to be late again. And seeing as Red hadn't come home last night, she decided it would most probably be her crawling back in from a drunken night on the town. Something she definitely didn't have time for.

To her surprise, Delta opened the door to an Authority dressed in his full white riot gear. The design of the helmets Authorities wore meant you could not see their faces but they could see yours. A feature that automatically made an onlooker feel unsettled. Generally aggressive and uncommunicative, Authorities were terrifying to the people of The Shell. It was extremely rare for them to pay someone's level a visit. This instantly made Delta feel uneasy.

"Oh, hello sir. Can I help you?" she asked cautiously.

"I'm looking for Red, is she here?" the Authority spoke quickly and abruptly.

"No, I don't think so. I don't think she came home last night," Delta replied sounding confused. "Is there a problem?"

"Maybe. Look, it's just extremely important that I find her," the man replied. "Can I come in?" Delta was startled that the Authority even asked.

"Yes, yes of course. Hang on, let me double check for you," Delta said inviting the man in and walking towards Red's bedroom. "I'll call her if she's not here."

Kyan waited in the living room, looking at a photo of Red and Delta that sat in an old-fashioned frame on a ledge in the wall. The two girls had their faces pressed beside each other and were grinning with their teeth on show. They looked a couple of years younger. Kyan suddenly felt uneasy as he stood in the two young girls' home, dressed in full Authority uniform.

Delta came back into the room. "I'm afraid she's not there, sir. I've tried calling her too but she didn't answer, would you like me to give you her number?"

"No, it's fine," Kyan answered blankly, impersonating an

Authority as best he could. "We have that already."

"Would you mind if I ask what this is about?" Delta asked in the most passive voice she could manage. "She's not in trouble, is she?"

"We hope not," he replied. "I will need you to help me find her, though."

Delta nodded automatically.

"Do you have any idea where she might be?" Kyan asked.

"There's a couple of places I know, yes," Delta said thinking instantly about the greenhouse Red adored but how she wouldn't be able to take an Authority there. "I reckon there's someone we could ask though, which might lead us to her quicker."

Kyan nodded and signalled towards the door, before simply saying: "Take me to them."

Delta left her level with the man she thought was an Authority and was shown to his pod. She knew that missing work could result in her losing her wages for an entire week – but what could she do? Refusing to help an Authority could cost Delta her life. The pair made their way towards the home of Ethan, who in that moment lay gagged and tied up on his bathroom floor.

* * *

As Red maneuvered her therapist's pod closer towards the vessels she'd once been transported down to The Shell in, she noticed the presence of Authorities patrolling the area grow stronger. She kept her head low so that only a glimpse of her shaved head could be seen from outside the vehicle.

She hadn't been this close to the exit zone since she first arrived in the United Underworld, but she'd studied the route ever since a copy of a map of the sector had been made available on Shareflow. Something she imagined Ivan Spencer must have both loathed and feared. She'd also memorised the journey they'd taken through the Docklands the night Ethan had taken her for a drink.

In his televised broadcasts, Ivan Spencer would tell the inhabitants of The Shell that going above the water and back on to what was left of the land would be far too dangerous and put everyone's lives at risk. But Red put this down to something very different. In her mind, she knew what the president was really afraid of: what could happen if there was an uprising. If the people of the United Underworld decided to revolt.

Red had longed for a revolution for so long. She'd read many books, both fiction and nonfiction, about people coming together and fighting back against the powers that be. She'd played out scenarios many times in her mind where the citizens of The Shell took their weapons – be it rayguns, flames or simply their fists – and wiped out Ivan Spencer and his regime.

But this was not fiction and it wasn't the past. The truth was, there would be no flames in the air without flames in people's hearts. And, seeing as no one seemed to share the same passion, resentment and rage towards the government that Red did, she decided there would be no uprising anytime soon. She put this down to the fact people were either too afraid or too stupid to realise what was going on around them. This is why Red decided she would have to be the revolution herself. She'd have to be the flame everyone else was too scared to light within themselves.

Red parked the pod in a quiet area that she knew was near the exit zone. She was so close it was as if she could smell the outside world already, but this was just the beginning of her mission. The hardest part was yet to come. Her heart started to beat faster and she could feel her breathing become more rapid.

The eager young woman checked to ensure that she had everything in her rucksack; food supplies, plenty of water, and a first aid kit. She'd hidden her switchblade up her sleeve while her taser was placed in the side of Ethan's boot, which was about three sizes too big for her. She knew she wasn't going to get very far in them, but they would have to do at this stage.

She also still had her connector, which had remained switched off since the night before to ensure the government couldn't track her. There was no way she could let Delta know what she was doing. She knew how much her friend would disapprove of it. Additionally, she didn't want to get her involved with any unnecessary danger. After all, this was her battle to fight alone.

Red heard a movement from outside. From the corner of her eye she noticed an Authority moving closer towards the pod. She ducked down, grabbed her rucksack and moved into the lower back compartment of the vehicle. She pulled the taser out from the inside of her boot and kept very still. It was a thin, metallic tube that emitted a strong shock of laser energy when its sensor was tapped. It was enough to stun, or even make the recipient lose consciousness when hit by the ray. Red found it unsettling how all therapists were told to carry one of these dangerous weapons. But then, patients were not always as obliging as Ivan Spencer would hope. If Ethan had been any other therapist, he would have already used his taser on Red by now. Just like her last therapist had tried.

Red could hear the Authority getting closer.

"Who's there?" his muffled voice spoke out from inside his helmet.

Red knew she would have to act fast. With both hands, she grabbed the handles of the side door of the pod and manually pushed it open with all of her strength. As the door made impact with the Authority it made a loud crunching sound and sent him flying off his feet.

Red then grabbed the taser, leapt out from the pod and landed on top of the Authority. She sent a painful shock pulsating into the man's veins as she held the weapon against his neck, pressing her thumb down on the sensor. Electric-blue bolts shot through the man's body, making him drop his raygun to the floor as he cried out in pain. Red took her finger off the sensor and reached down to grab the lethal weapon the Authority had dropped. As she did, a sharp sensation entered her own body sending her flying to the floor and landing on her back. The raygun was still charged with current from the taser.

After a few seconds, the Authority stood upright and reached for his weapon. Red quickly pulled her switchblade from her sleeve pocket and sent it soaring into her opponent's hand, slicing straight through. As he screamed out in pain, Red grabbed the man's raygun, lifted it towards his head and shot out a small yet thick blast of energy that went hurtling towards him. Sparks flew and a surge of blood sprayed against the concrete floor before the man fell down. Dead.

Red drew back a quick gasp of air as it dawned on her what she'd done. She'd never killed anyone before and despite the fact it was an anonymous Authority, she felt an instant rush of guilt and disgust with herself. *That could have been someone's father*, she thought. But before she could let her humanity sweep in any further, she knew she would have to hide the evidence before any other Authorities arrived.

She held the back of her hand against the lifeless body for a few seconds to ensure it wasn't still charged with energy. His burnt white uniform felt hot, but she didn't get a shock from touching it. Without another thought, Red used all of her strength and scooped the dead man up and pulled him into the pod. Once inside, she removed his helmet to be met with the face of a young man with a shaved head. He couldn't have been much older than twenty-five. His skin had already turned a dull greyish colour as the blood drained from his body. His eyes were closed, as if he were sleeping.

Red felt for the young man, mostly because he had been caught up in working for the government at such a young age. But she couldn't waste any more time, so she had to try as hard as she could to disconnect from her emotions as she removed the rest of the deceased Authority's uniform.

* * *

Red's third earliest memory of the ocean was on her eighth birthday: the day her father died. Her mother had never told her the full story about how this happened, just that he had got himself into some trouble that involved his work. Red's mother would always tell her daughter how he had a rebellious streak, a darker side that yearned to disobey and defy convention. This would get the family in trouble at times, considering the fact that he worked for the government.

Although Red never properly got to know her father, or find out what really happened the day her mother told her he would never be coming home, she felt somehow that she related to him more than anyone. That rebellious streak had obviously passed right down into Red's own fiery blood and she promised herself that day that she would make him proud.

That same afternoon, when she should have been at home blowing out eight sparkly little candles on a cake with her mother and father, she instead spent her birthday alone on the beach staring into the crashing waves. The unforgiving water, in all its ruthless glory, crashing against the shore. There she sat motionless, not even a tear shed. She just gazed into the water and down at the piles of broken shells beneath her feet.

It was on this day, when the innocence of her childhood faded away like grains of sand blowing away from a dune, that Red became grimly aware of mortality. Aware of what it was to stop and be no more. She looked down at the thousands of broken shells. Sharp and empty like abandoned houses. She realised how they had once all belonged to tiny living organisms that roamed the earth's sea bed. The beach she'd once seen as so beautiful all of a sudden looked like a graveyard for thousands of small dead creatures.

But within moments she had another thought, on that cold and grim winter's day. The shells that lay before her, discarded like dead skin, were not skeletons left to decay. They were armour. Armour left to honour the life of what had gone before and be viewed as beautiful and infinite. She realised that shells were the legacy of the life beneath the ocean.

This was exactly the memory that entered Red's head, all those years later, as she walked towards the exit of the United Underworld clothed in the dead Authority's uniform. *This was his armour*, she thought. *Now it'll be mine.* She would honour the first man she'd ever killed, as misled as he was, by fighting for what she thought was good and morally right in the shell he once wore.

If she died trying, this armour would be her own legacy. Left as a reminder to whoever found it that someone dared to rise up and go against the grain. To rise up against the machine. But then again, she had no intention to die trying.

As Red stepped towards the exit zone that led to whatever was left of the world above, she took a moment to think of her father. Despite her lack of faith, she convinced herself that he was watching her every move. That he was standing proudly in her corner.

NINE

While Red walked towards the exit of The Shell clothed in Authority gear, someone else who shared her thirst for justice was disguised in the very same uniform. Kyan had been waiting with Delta outside of Ethan's level for at least ten minutes before they started to consider breaking in.

"If we wait just a little bit longer I'm sure he'll be back," said Delta.

"I'm worried we don't even have a few minutes to spare," replied Kyan in a tone that Delta felt was surprisingly compassionate for an Authority. "We're going in."

Moments later, Kyan used the weight of his raygun to break down the therapist's door. The pair burst into the flat to be met with nothing but an empty room.

"There's no one here," said Delta, blankly.

"Check the other rooms," Kyan replied, already marching into Ethan's bedroom.

As Delta tried to open the locked bathroom door, she realised that she could hear a muffled sound coming from inside.

"He-hello?" she stuttered quietly.

Kyan came storming in behind her and smashed the door down with his weapon. The unlikely pair were met by Ethan lying tied up and gagged on the floor, dressed only in his underwear.

"Oh my god, Ethan!" Delta cried out as she ran over to him. As Kyan untied his hands, Delta tore the tape off his mouth. Ethan let out a loud gasp for air, before managing to croak out a simple sentence that was barely loud enough to be a whisper:

"We've got to find Red."

Meanwhile, Red was stepping aboard the shuttle that was scheduled to leave The Shell and be sent above the ocean. She'd followed in line through the confined corridors that led to the vessels with a group of Authorities, the same way she'd done all those years ago when she was first transported down to the United Underworld. She kept quiet and tried to mirror the mechanical way they walked. Once inside, she slowed her pace down to lose them and quickly crept into an empty part of the vessel. It was then she realised she would have to vacate the vehicle before it arrived above the water.

As Red felt the vessel start to move, she slipped between a few cargo crates and kept as still and quiet as she could. When the vessel picked up speed, a deafening hum echoed off the decade-old leaking walls of the vehicle. Just above her head was a small fire escape hatch. This would be her exit when the time was right.

She knew that the trip from The Shell to the nearest bay took less than twenty-five minutes, so she would have to climb out at least a minute before it arrived. If she escaped too early, she would risk being too far out at sea and too far below the water's surface. She would drown. And if she waited much longer she would end up having to leave with the other Authorities and risk getting caught. At least if she swam to the surface, she would buy herself a bit more time to suss out the situation in the Overworld, although she feared what she would discover.

Red shuddered at the thought of getting caught. She could imagine Ivan Spencer's face. His beady eyes staring into hers. Looking her up and down. At her shaved head, bruised body and battered Authority uniform. Perhaps it even still had some blood left on it from the man she shot and killed. The man who had died serving the government he believed in.

Perhaps the satisfaction she would get from seeing the expression on Ivan Spencer's face would be worth her fate. Still, she decided she would prefer to risk dying from the toxic fumes the asteroid had left behind than be subjected to whatever cruel torture the president would have in store for her. He would not tolerate being outsmarted by someone from The Shell. Least of all a young woman.

Red's thoughts were interrupted as she heard the sound of steps drawing closer. She ducked down and hid herself behind the crate, holding her breath with fear and to stop herself from making any sound. Within moments, she realised that the steps had been walking in another direction and the coast was clear. But this, combined with the fact that the vessel must have been mere minutes away from reaching the water's surface, was enough to persuade her to make an abrupt exit from the vehicle and swim the rest of the way herself. She decided that even if she drowned, at least she would get to feel fresh water against her skin one last time.

Red climbed up onto the crate she'd been hiding behind, reached up for the fire exit's wheel handle and hoisted her body towards it. She had to use every ounce of strength within her body to lift herself up towards the door, before she managed to hook the tips of her boots into the ridges within the vessel's wall. Then, using all of her force, she managed to twist the wheel around until it released the door and sent a huge wave of water gushing in.

Without pausing to think, Red forced the hatch open and pulled herself through the rapid stream of seawater before the Authorities had a chance to check what was happening. She was catapulted from the vehicle as the door slammed behind her and the vessel continued to speed through the ocean. As she was sent on a dizzying spin through the open water, she hoped the sheer volume in the vessel had disguised the noise of her escape. *But what will they think when they see all the water?* Red worried.

But there was no time to be afraid. Red needed to focus on holding her breath for as long as possible as she figured out which way to swim towards the ocean's surface. She pulled off her helmet to prevent it from weighing her head down, but kept it tightly within her grasp. The determined young woman was in agony as she started to swim. She was sure she'd been cut by the sharp metal edges of the escape hatch as she forced her body through it.

Red swam as fast as she could. As blood pumped around her body, the pain subsided. She realised that she hadn't been injured after all. It was the freezing cold water against her skin that felt cutting. But that didn't matter. It was real and it was natural. Through her anguish, Red felt whole and she felt alive.

As she swam further and further towards the surface, Red could see a large beacon of light pouring down through the water. She felt a surge of relief, as she wouldn't have been able to hold her breath for much longer. Could it have been the large robots that Ivan Spencer was using to rebuild what was left of Earth's land? Or could it have been the sun?

Within seconds, Red burst through the water's surface like a bird hatching from an egg. Water splashing out in different directions like pieces of the egg's shell splintering away. As she drew in a large breath and opened her eyes, two incredible things dawned on her simultaneously.

One was that the air she breathed in was as fresh as it had been the day she climbed into the vessel to be transported to The Shell. The other was that standing before her was land. Trees, shrubs and fields. As green, lush and beautiful as they were the day humanity had been sent beneath the ocean.

Much more began to dawn on Red, in an epiphany of the greatest kind. Like a person spending their entire life in a coma, only to be awoken suddenly. Like a person spending their life blind, only to be unexpectedly awarded the gift of sight.

She realised that the earth, the beautiful earth that she'd so missed and longed for, stood as tall as it ever did. She felt the pang of disgust, horror and sadness for all the years she – and all the other people who resided in The Shell – had been kept from the world and led to believe it was gone forever. People like Marcus, who never got to see natural light or feel fresh air on his face again.

She realised that the asteroid, if there had even been an asteroid, had not left the world in ruin the way Ivan Spencer and his regime had the inhabitants of The Shell believe.

Then finally, it dawned on Red that her mother – one of the only people left in the world that she truly cared for – could still be alive. The woman who had been taken from her on that awful day a decade ago. The woman she thought had turned to ashes after a giant burning rock hit the earth, like a pebble dropped on a grain of sand. Red's painful and endless mourning could have all been in vain. And could finally be about to end.

It was this thought, this hope rediscovered, that managed to pull Red's vision back into focus and provoke her blood to start pumping around her veins once more. She tied the Authority's mask to the side of her battered uniform and directed her eyes towards the industrial buildings on the land's bay and what looked like further buildings in the distance.

Without another thought of the dangers that might lay ahead, or the mysteries left to uncover, Red was filled with both bravery and caution as she began to swim slowly towards the land's surface.

PART TWO

INTO THE ASHES

TEN

Rough waves slammed against Red's sides like exploding rainclouds. She kept her vision firmly fixed on the beckoning land before her. Could she really be seeing this? Surely it would turn out to be a mirage.

But the closer she got to her destination, the more she realised that her eyes weren't deceiving her. It had to all be a lie. There was no way Ivan Spencer and his regime could have rebuilt the world this much. Not after seeing the images the televised transmissions had shown. The damage the asteroid had left behind had been far too immense.

These images had relayed to the inhabitants of The Shell that the asteroid had not only destroyed all of the cities across the world, but the forests and mountains too. Colossal craters had supposedly been left across the land, while tsunamis and poisonous gases had destroyed whatever life had been spared from the asteroid's blow.

So if this really had been the case, how could the government have rebuilt the damage done to the point where it looked untouched? And even if they had, why had this been hidden from the people of the United Underworld for so long?

There were too many questions flying through Red's head, just like the waves crashing against the sides of her clinical white Authority uniform as she swam. She would have to try and tune them out and stay focused if she was going to reach the land alive. She'd already begun to grow tired and her destination still seemed so far away.

There was also the bigger issue of what she would actually do if she even made it to land alive. Despite being dressed as an Authority, she wouldn't be able to hide her true identity forever. The government would have probably been alerted that she was coming after she'd allowed a wave of water to be sent gushing into the vessel she'd escaped from.

Or perhaps Ethan had woken from being drugged, broken free from the rope she'd tied him up with and notified the government about what she'd done. Red felt sad as she thought of him. Someone who had shown her genuine care and affection, despite her suspicions. How had she repaid him? By betraying him in a way that was both callous and potentially lethal.

It would have been hard for Red to have even denied to herself that she had feelings for Ethan, which was partly why she'd made the decision to risk her life and escape The Shell. Even if she could truly trust him, there was no way she could trust the people he was working for. There was no way she could have had any sort of relationship with her therapist. It would have been like having a relationship with part of Ivan

Spencer's corrupt machine.

Besides, any sort of guilt or remorse that Red felt for drugging Ethan, stealing his uniform and locking him up inside his bathroom, was soon forgotten when she reminded herself what had finally spurred her on to escape The Shell in the first place. Just picturing the face of Marcus as he took his last breath was enough to make her choke. Enough to stir the emotions locked within her chest. Like frantic bats flying through an echoic cave. Just the thought of how Marcus had never got to see trees or the sky again was enough to make her blood boil. Particularly when she realised these natural wonders had been there all along.

Red used her sentiments and adrenaline to fight her way through her lethargy and continued to swim against the ruthless waves. She was going to make it to the shore alive, no matter what might be waiting for her on arrival.

In the time Red had spent fleeing the vessel, swimming to the ocean's surface and making her way towards land, three people from very different backgrounds had come together to share one unified mission. To rescue her.

Delta, who sat cross-legged with her curly chestnut locks tied back to keep them from falling onto her face, had gone quiet as she listened closely to what the two men in the room were saying. She had her connector in her hands, but she had it switched to silent. She planned to ignore any calls she would inevitably receive from her colleagues and Xavier.

As much as Xavier got along with Red, there was no way he would agree with his girlfriend's decision to risk her life for her friend's reckless behaviour. As far as he was concerned, Red was already a lost cause and Delta was better off without her. Although he had only been dating Delta for a few months, he would quite happily have moved in with her full time and seen Red and her newly-acquired stray cat move out. Like Delta, he had suggested to Red that she join them both working at the Reactor. But Red was having none of it. At this point she could have been putting all of their lives in danger.

There was simply no way Delta could have spoken to him about the situation. She could barely get her own thoughts together, let alone have someone else's doubts and assumptions cloud her judgment. She disagreed with what Red had done and was afraid for her own life, but there was no way she could let her friend go without even attempting to save her. Delta was almost certain that even if Red had managed to escape The Shell, she surely would have choked on the poisonous gases in the Overworld. But she had to remain optimistic.

Delta listened closely to what Ethan was saying, though she could barely piece his sentences together through all the static noise in her head. She stared straight ahead at his youthful face that was both worn and hopeful.

Ethan sat at the table in his kitchenette opposite the mysterious Authority trying to devise a plan. He had true feelings for his patient. He cared for her deeply. Apart from Delta and Marcus, Ethan was also the only person to get as close as he had to Red's heart. Or at least he thought he had. He was willing to look past what she'd done to him. He understood her actions. He understood her anger and ambition to escape, but he also understood that she might be in trouble.

As much as Ethan had always defended Ivan Spencer when

talking to Red, deep down he had his own doubts and concerns about the regime. He himself wondered why the government had been stalling with its developments in the New Overworld. He hadn't wanted to fuel Red's worries, as he knew how much she distrusted the government already. He wished he'd spoken to her sooner. Perhaps she wouldn't have tried to escape if he'd just voiced his own concerns.

Concerns like: why were there no legal trials in The Shell? Or how could people just go missing, never to be seen or heard from again? Just like what had happened to Red's previous therapist. And others who had failed their tasks. Or Ethan's biggest concern that he'd never been able to truly get his head around. Something that made him identify with Red more than many others. He wondered why accidents had been allowed to occur that led to groups of people being left above the ground when the asteroid hit. People like his younger sister, Leyla. Or Red's mother.

Scratching the side of his shaved head and looking through his pale-blue eyes at the Authority who sat opposite, Ethan wondered if the stranger could be trusted. Although the Authority had convinced both himself and Delta that he had decided to revolt against the government and surrender his life to saving Red, it still made Ethan feel uneasy that he couldn't see the mysterious man's face through his battered dome-shaped helmet. All the therapist could see was his own discoloured and nervous-looking reflection staring back.

But the mystery man argued that he was the pair's sole hope of finding Red as he claimed to be the only one who had actually been to the New Overworld. Most Authorities did have access above the ocean as they were usually stationed either at the arrival bay of the Overworld or the exit zone of The Shell, keeping watch. This meant it was very likely the masked stranger knew roughly what to expect if they even managed to escape The Shell.

But in reality, the person behind the Authority's mask did not know the truth about the asteroid at all. And if he had, he would have ensured that every single inhabitant of The Shell was made aware of it by this point. This was because Kyan, although technically employed by the government, was still ultimately the face behind the only whistleblowing website in The Shell. So if he were to discover that the world above remained just as intact as it had before the supposed *Day of Judgement*, he would be making a rather important leak to Shareflow.

Kyan had no intention of revealing his true identity to Ethan or Delta. Despite understanding that all three of them were risking their lives even contemplating devising a plan to rescue Red, he was still concerned that he would be recognised and uncovered by Ivan Spencer, who wouldn't take kindly to being deceived by one of the people who worked so closely with him. He particularly wouldn't be amused if he found out that this man was also the brains behind Shareflow, a website he and his regime had worked so hard to try and shut down.

Both Ethan and Kyan knew they would have to convince Delta that she couldn't come with them. They were aware she would have to return to her work at the Reactor to prevent other people from asking questions if Red even stood a chance of survival. As much as it pained Ethan to even think of it, he himself doubted that there was much hope left for the life of the woman he cared for so deeply.

But at this point in time, all three of them simply sat in silence. They tried to read each other's thoughts as Kyan sketched out the route he and Ethan would need to take once they made it above the ocean. All three completely unaware of the truth about the asteroid. How the Apocalypse had not only been the biggest hoax of the twenty-second century — but in the history of humanity. Or how, as they spoke, Red was battling against the ruthless waves of the Atlantic. Feeling just as afraid of reaching land as she was of drowning trying to get there.

* * *

As Red got closer to land, she realised that she would have to change her direction to avoid arriving at the bay where the vessels from The Shell pulled into. She could make out a small cluster of industrial-looking buildings to one side of the bay. On the other there was a stretch of surprisingly-lush woodland.

Behind all the greenery stood the tallest buildings she'd ever seen, some of which were exceptionally wide. It was unlike any of the architecture Red remembered as a child. The designs looked different, more contemporary and complex. Or perhaps she'd simply forgotten what the world had looked like.

Above all this, the sky was as blue as the way Red remembered Ethan's eyes. The clouds like cotton wool. The air felt bitter but not freezing, hinting that it could be a crisp autumn day. This was something Red had not experienced in a very long time. She was used to the constant muggy feeling of The Shell. It wasn't sweltering down there. It just had constant uncomfortable warmth that felt musky and unsurprisingly synthetic.

Most citizens of the United Underworld had also lost track of what month it was, let alone the season. All time morphed into one continuous twenty-four-hour cycle of unnatural heat and occasional showers of artificial rain.

Red decided her best bet would be to make her way to the woodland where she would hide out. This would at least buy her enough time to recover from the gruelling swim before she worked out what her next move would be.

In what she realised must have been somewhere between mid to late afternoon, Red began to swim towards the beckoning greenery of the woodland. A giant seagull flew above her head letting out a distinctive squawk that reminded her of being by the seaside in her youth.

The sound of the bird, as well as the schools of tiny silver fish that swam past her, sparked something else in the young woman's mind. Something incredible.

There was still life on earth.

If Ivan Spencer really had been telling the truth about the asteroid, why hadn't it wiped out the birds and the small fish at the sea's surface? But at this point, it didn't matter. As she listened to the loud cries of the seagull above, Red took a moment to rest and simply enjoy the nostalgia of her childhood by the sea. She was finally home.

* * *

"I want to come too," said Delta, with surprising determination. This was a new side to her. A side that even she was not familiar with.

"No, it's too dangerous," Ethan's reply was firm and sincere. He felt it would be far too risky for Delta to join him and the Authority in escaping The Shell as she had too many connections. Such as Xavier and her colleagues at the Reactor. They would already be wondering where she was and it wouldn't take long before the Authorities would be notified that she was missing. At least Red's job no longer existed.

"But I can't just sit around down here knowing that my best friend is up there choking on poisonous gases," Delta continued, visibly upset.

"With all due respect, ma'am," said Kyan, "I think it's best you stay down here and return to work. It would be too suspicious if you came with us to the Overworld. Your best option is to act normal and keep anyone else who might notice Red's absence distracted."

It dawned on Delta that Xavier would be due to meet her from work in an hour or so. If she left at this point, she might be able to get away with appearing like she'd been at the Reactor all day. It would be easy to distract him from Red's disappearance. He would revel in the fact that they would have the flat to themselves. Delta realised that this option, as difficult as it would be, was the right thing to do.

"Ok, I understand," she said, disappointedly. "You guys go ahead, but please stay in touch." Delta paused for a moment, glaring at both Ethan and the mystery Authority one by one to put emphasis on her next sentence:

"And please... bring her back."

Ethan and Kyan nodded in unison, not wanting to make the promise out loud. Delta left her connector code with the two men and set off towards the Reactor to meet her lover.

* * *

By the time Red reached land, she was physically and mentally exhausted. Instead of jumping from the water the way she'd planned – running across the pebbles and heading straight to the woodland to wrap her arms around a tree – she was instead washed up on the shore like a dead fish. Her body slammed against the rocks with a loud thump.

Breathing deeply, Red slipped in and out of consciousness as she lay against the tiny stones on the beach. It was bitterly cold, but she could feel slight warmth from the late afternoon sun. It felt heavenly. As did the fresh sea air she inhaled and exhaled through her mouth, which felt as dry as sandpaper. The waves splashed against her legs like buckets of water being thrown over her repeatedly.

Within a few minutes, Red realised how dangerous it was for her to be laying on the beach and that she would have to get up and lose herself within the forest. Using every last bit of strength she could muster, she pulled herself from the sodden stones beneath her body. And for the first time since leaving the vessel, she stood on her feet.

Standing in front of her, the forest was enchanting. Like a setting from one of the fairy tales she'd read as a child. Even as a young girl living in the Old World, Red had never been to a forest. They had become few and far between in the later part of the twenty-first century as the population rose and the world became more and more urban.

Red dreamt of places like this all her life. Places filled with natural tones like green and brown. Not a steely grey in sight. Where colourful birds sang to each other as they flew and unusual insects crawled along the earth. It looked like an ethereal paradise, inviting her in. A Utopia. One she and the other residents of The Shell had been starved of. The thought made the tiny shaved hairs on Red's scalp stand up as she shuddered.

As if in a trance, Red began to step towards the natural wonderland.

In the time Red took to wash up on the shore and begin to make her way towards the forest, Ethan and Kyan were debating the best way to set out and find her. Aside from government officials and Authorities, no one was permitted to enter the New Overworld. Not even therapists and paramedics, despite their close link to Ivan Spencer's regime.

"Well, I won't have a problem, of course," said Kyan. "But we're going to have to get you some gear sorted."

Ethan had changed into a spare therapist uniform he owned, but he would have to be disguised as an Authority when he attempted to escape The Shell.

Seeing as Kyan had access to some of these uniforms at the United Underworld Studios, he knew he would be able to pick one up for his new accomplice. As well as this, he had a shift that evening that he really couldn't afford to miss.

"I'll be able to get you one tonight, if that's not too late?" Kyan asked rhetorically.

"That would be great, thank you!" said Ethan enthusiastically. He still wasn't sure if he could completely trust the Authority. He was even worried about the fact that he could be an undercover spy working for the government. But he was willing to take the risk to save Red's life.

"Ok, good. Shall we meet again tonight at midnight, so I can give it to you then?" Kyan asked before Ethan nodded in agreement. "Then we can work out how we're going to save the girl," he added assertively. Kyan left Ethan's flat and rushed home to get changed for work.

Ethan continued to sit at his kitchen table in silence, waiting. He knew he would have to try and eat something and get some rest, but he had no idea how he could. He inhaled a deep breath of warm, musky air as his mind began to wander. The girl he had begun to fall for so intensely was somewhere out there in the dangerous Overworld, alone. Or she'd died trying to escape.

He exhaled.

ELEVEN

Stepping into the forest felt like stepping through the gates of Heaven. Red's eyes darted from tree to bush as she walked slowly through the beautiful woodland. She was still fully clothed in the Authority uniform. The helmet felt heavy against her newly-shaved head. It was an indescribable sensation to be back on her feet after the brutal swim to shore. To be walking on natural land. Perhaps she really had drowned and gone to Heaven.

Red took each step slowly, trying to keep as quiet as she possibly could. She had no idea who or what she might come across in the mysterious woodland. She could hear the faint sound of crickets in the bushes. Or were they frogs? It didn't matter. Either way, more life. She could also hear a roaring sound from her stomach. She was starving. Unsurprising really, considering the amount of energy she'd burnt off swimming to land.

While Red usually refused to eat insects in The Shell, she knew that she wouldn't have much choice when setting off on her mission. She needed all the protein she could get to remain strong. She'd packed dozens of dried-out crickets, locusts and beetles in her bag, as well as all the grains and nuts she could get her hands on.

Red quickly realised that catching and eating insects and reptiles would be a far better way to gain energy than consuming the food supply she'd already packed. After all, she'd expected to be walking across an ash-filled wasteland by now.

But then, another thought occurred to her. The inhabitants of The Shell may have lived off insects, but Red had access to an enormous woodland full of life. Who knew what she could find if she went hunting? Besides, she'd just emerged from a bay that had tiny silver fish swimming on its surface. Perhaps they'd be easy to catch and cook.

The idea of walking back to the bay worried Red. She'd already started making her way through the forest and it could be dangerous to turn back. She decided she would look for something to eat on land. She knew she would have to act fast as the sun had begun to set and very soon the woodland would be plunged into darkness.

Red pulled her switchblade out from her boot, tightened the straps of her rucksack and began to meander through the wild bushes of the forest. She checked her connector for the first time since she arrived on land, before realising that it was no longer working. Water must have seeped into the motherboard as she swam to the ocean's surface. She threw the small piece of broken equipment into her rucksack.

There was no hope of communicating with her friends in The Shell at this point. Red thought for a moment about what she'd given up, but she quickly reminded herself of the horror she'd left behind. Her attention was then turned fully back to her hunger.

Remaining as quiet as she could, Red began to realise that she could see and hear life everywhere she looked. Thick spider webs between blades of grass. Different types of birds were fluttering above her head. Tiny ants and other insects scurried past her feet. But it was the squirrels scrambling along tree branches that really got Red's mouth watering. In an instant, the thought of catching tiny silver fish was forgotten. She decided that one of the chestnut-coloured tree dwellers would be the most delicious option to have for dinner.

Walking slowly, Red approached a tree where she saw one of the small creatures nibbling on an acorn while perched on an eye-level branch. She knew how to survive on the bleak and industrial streets of The Shell, but she had no experience in hunting in the natural world. She imagined it would take a few attempts before she would even manage to catch one of the little critters.

Red took off the bulky Authority helmet and her beaten-up rucksack. She placed each item quietly beside her feet, being careful not to breathe too heavily. Her eyes remained fixed on the squirrel, which had stopped munching on the acorn. Had it heard her? Perhaps it sensed that she was coming. Red quietly took a couple more steps forward before she stepped on a twig that created a loud snap. The squirrel froze, before turning around and darting into a round hole in the side of the tree trunk to hide.

Red suddenly pitied the little animal. This was too easy. The squirrel had practically trapped itself in the tree, the same way humanity was trapped inside The Shell. She shuddered at the thought of being like Ivan Spencer. Playing God. No, this was different. This was survival. Survival of the fittest and she had to be strong. She'd come this far. She knew she had to be a fighter if she wanted to even consider surviving.

Without another thought or doubt, Red leapt forward towards the hole in the tree trunk and plunged her switchblade into the side of the squirrel's throat. She let out a loud cry as its blood sprayed onto her. A war cry. She felt barbaric, animalistic, primitive, but none of this mattered anymore. She was hungry and needed to eat.

Red pulled the squirrel out from the tree trunk and made sure it was dead. It occurred to her that she'd killed the animal with one single blow. This bleak realisation reminded her of the fragility of life. How the Authority had died just as easily as the squirrel. How the squirrel had died as instantly as the insects she'd killed prior to her mission. Life was precious, but also feeble. She couldn't allow herself to be fragile. She had to keep moving.

With the fruit of her hunt in hand, Red began collecting twigs and logs, which she would use to build a fire. She was concerned how the smell or sight of smoke could draw the attention of whoever might be out there, beyond the woodland. But she had no choice. She needed to eat. It was dark by this point and she also needed to rest. She planned to cook the entire squirrel, eat half of it and save the other half for breakfast. She had no idea if she'd even be able to sleep, but she knew she had to try. She hadn't slept since she left Ethan's flat and it had been an extremely long day. She was beyond exhausted. It was essential that she rebuilt her strength before continuing her journey to wherever she was going.

But Red herself didn't know where she was heading. As she began to create a pile of twigs and branches she'd collected, she realised how much of her mission had been spontaneous and unplanned. She recognised the fact that if the ocean really had been poisoned from gasses released by the asteroid, she might have even been killed swimming to shore. That was the risk Red had been willing to take.

The irony of the situation, Red pondered, *is that in some ways Ivan Spencer saved my life simply by lying about the Apocalypse.* She shook her head with disbelief at her own thoughts. *But if he hadn't made the whole lie up in the first place, I would've had no reason to risk my life.* Red decided it must have been her hunger and exhaustion clouding her thoughts. She also decided that she had to try and block the situation out of her mind. At least at this stage, to focus on what she was doing.

Once satisfied with the small yet substantial pile of twigs and branches she'd collected, Red sat down cross-legged and began to rub two dried-out twigs together. Although she had the laser taser in her bag, she wanted to preserve its energy for as long as possible, seeing that there'd be no way to recharge it once it ran out of power.

Red smiled to herself at how earthy and ethereal the whole situation was. Almost otherworldly. She'd pretty much given up hope of stepping back onto the land above the ocean. Particularly land that hadn't been wiped away. The experience she was having was beyond surreal. She was in Utopia.

As if by magic, heat began to radiate from between the two twigs in Red's hands. Like a miracle. No electronic rays or power from The Shell's Reactor were needed. She was creating fire with her bare hands. Just like she'd read about in her antique printed books. It was the most beautiful and natural thing. It felt like a gift from God.

Before long, sparks began to ignite from the friction of the twigs. What followed was a small yet ferociously hot fire. The warmth of the flames felt amazing against Red's skin as they grew. The night had brought with it a bitter chill. She turned her switchblade on its side to skin the dead squirrel. She then tossed it into the fire.

The smell the animal extruded as it began to cook made Red's mouth instantly salivate. It smelled delicious. She started to fantasise about tearing pieces of the meat off, sucking the juices from them and chewing on the tender flesh before swallowing.

Before long, Red's fantasy became a reality. She stamped on the flames with the large Authority boots that were far too big for her, putting it out completely. It was so cold that she wished she could have kept the fire burning as she ate. Perhaps even as she slept. But it was too risky. She'd chosen a spot where the smoke had been shielded by a cluster of trees that towered above her, but there had still been the risk of someone smelling it.

Perhaps Authorities guarding the buildings she'd seen in

the distance would have noticed smoke gliding through the tops of the trees. Maybe even the Authorities patrolling the arrival bay would have seen it and signalled for others to come and investigate. But for now, Red had to banish those thoughts from her mind. Just like her concerns about the water that had got into the vessel when she escaped. She felt blessed to have come as far as she had. And it had only been a day.

Red set the laser taser she'd been keeping in her rucksack to standby. It produced a dim light, which was enough to use as a torch to allow her to see what she was eating. She knew that she would have to be careful with using the taser's energy. It wouldn't last forever and she was certain she'd be using it again. Red tore into the flesh of the roasted squirrel the same way a lion devours a lamb. She thought about how frightening she must have looked. On all fours in the darkness, her head shaved and eyes glazed over. She used her teeth to tear the meat off the dead animal's tiny bones.

She kept her promise to herself and left almost half of the squirrel to eat at dawn. She packed up her things, took a large swig from her flask of water and put her helmet back on. She decided that she would walk for at least another half hour or so, in case anyone had seen the smoke and decided to come and look for her while she slept. She came to the conclusion that she would search for a spot that felt tucked away and as hidden as possible.

As Red walked, she looked up and realised that she could see thousands of twinkling stars through the gaps in the trees. She could also see the milky moon, partly hidden by dark grey clouds. This was a sight she hadn't seen in a very long time, but something she'd never forgotten. There had barely been a day that went by when Red hadn't thought about the stars and the moon, as well as all of the other planets and mystery that existed out in the galaxy. Were there others like her, looking out into space in wonder? Were there others who had been forced to spend their lives living underneath the ocean? If oceans even existed on other planets.

Red wondered for a moment whether Ivan Spencer and his regime had come any closer to discovering life out in space. There had been minor discoveries over the years, new planets found that had been previously unknown. But still no sign of life. All of a sudden she felt very alone as she stared up into the darkness. The sky felt like a ceiling, like she was back in The Shell. The stars were like the bolts in the United Underworld's roof. She soon realised how stupid her thoughts were. Earth was nothing like The Shell. It was enormous and beautiful. Limitless and natural. Once again she was reminded of her newfound freedom and of all the life that surrounded her. She suddenly felt less alone.

Before long, Red came across a tree that had partly fallen over. On its side, the broken trunk had created a space underneath it that would be perfect for her to hide under as she slept. She considered the chances of the tree falling down and crushing her, but concluded they were slim and decided to risk it. It was very cold, but there was hardly any wind. Plus, the tree felt sturdy when she tried to give it a shake. She slipped underneath the trunk, turned her rucksack on its side to use as a pillow and shut her eyes.

Red's scrambled thoughts grew increasingly abstract and

drifted away like ghosts in the night as she fell into a deep sleep. She dreamt that she was being held in the arms of a hybrid of an angel and a copper beech tree. She dreamt she was being held in the arms of both her mother and her father. She'd never felt so safe.

TWELVE

Ethan's eyes opened abruptly. He shot upright with an instant feeling of shock and guilt. He checked the time. 06:33. How had he fallen asleep? How had he allowed himself to rest when Red's life was at stake or maybe already over? He climbed off the sofa and reached for his connector. One message from the mystery Authority:

I'M SORRY, I WON'T BE BACK TONIGHT. IT WAS TOO RISKY TO GET MY HANDS ON AN AUTHORITY UNIFORM. IT'S BEST WE BOTH REST FOR NOW, ANYWAY. I'M BUSY TODAY BUT WILL HEAD OVER THIS EVENING WITH YOUR DISGUISE. TRUST ME.

Ethan clenched his fists with frustration. So he would have to sit around and wait for the mystery Authority to arrive before he would be able to go after Red? And how did he know he really could trust this stranger? It seemed like a convenient story that he wasn't able to get hold of another uniform. Surely he owned a spare? Ethan decided pretty swiftly that he had to come up with another plan. He simply wasn't prepared to wait.

It was then Ethan remembered he had a lunch meeting with a government official about Red's progress. Typical. What the hell was he going to say? *Sorry, I failed the task. I fell for Red and she's now either dead or somewhere lost in the Overworld.* He would end up magically disappearing, just like the previous therapist who had tried to get inside Red's brain.

Ethan had always found it strange how the government had focused so much time on following Red's progress. As much as it pained him to even think it, why hadn't they just killed her by this point if she was so defiant? She wouldn't be the first young woman to go missing in the shadowy streets of the United Underworld. Ethan shuddered at the thought.

But at this point in time, it didn't matter. He decided that if anything, this meeting could be his meal ticket out of The Shell. If he played his cards right. He had approximately five hours to come up with a plan. And he had already begun to devise one.

Kyan hadn't been lying when he said it had been too dangerous to get his hands on a uniform. He had gone to the United Underworld Studios, but had somehow forgotten about the amount of Authorities that guard every single entrance to the government-owned building. He'd messaged Ethan, gone home and slept. As Ethan woke up, Kyan was also getting up and preparing to go to work as normal. If he didn't, it would become too suspicious. He knew he had the following day off, so he would use this time to try and escape to the Overworld with Ethan.

But little did he know that as he travelled to the United Underworld Studios in his pod, Ethan was planning to ask the government official he was meeting if he could be granted an exclusive tour of the New Overworld. And he wasn't prepared to take no for an answer.

* * *

It dawned on Red that she was awake a minute or two before she opened her eyes. She knew she was still lying underneath the tree trunk, which felt strangely comforting. She felt relieved to even be alive. But she was also aware that she wasn't particularly safe. *What if there are Authorities waiting for me outside?* Red's thoughts were interrupted by the sensation of something crawling across her face.

Red screamed and jerked upright, banging her face against the tree trunk. Whatever large insect had been making its way across her cheek fell off and scuttled away. She rolled sideways onto the soft ground and landed on her back. She opened her eyes. The daylight was breathtaking. It was a cloudy day and the sky was a blanket of pale grey, no blue in sight. But it didn't matter that it wasn't sunny like the days that stuck out in her memory. She was safe. She was alive and she was in the Overworld.

Red actually longed for the rain. She longed to feel natural drops of water against her face, unlike the artificial ones that were released in The Shell. But she had no time to sit around gazing at the clouds. She needed to get up, scoff down the rest of the squirrel she'd savagely murdered the night before and continue on her journey. Wherever that led.

Although Red still appeared to be alone, she was afraid someone would come after her soon. She sat down with her raygun by her side, ready to attack if the moment came. She devoured the rest of the squirrel, then packed her bag and put her Authority helmet on once more. It was time to continue walking. From what she'd seen as she swam towards the land, the towering buildings were not too far away. She expected to see them poking over the trees anytime soon. But the distance could have been deceptive. She really had no idea how far the woodland would continue.

And even if she did manage to make it to the buildings alive, she had no idea what to expect once she got there. Or what she planned to do on arrival. All she knew was: she'd come this far. She couldn't turn back now. She'd probably be killed if she even tried. She had to trust her instincts and keep moving forward. She had to move.

Red had barely been walking through the bushes for a few minutes before her prayers were answered, and the skies opened. Large drops of rain began to crash down against the grass-stained Authority uniform she wore. She removed the heavy dome-shaped helmet and allowed the water to splash against her face.

She took a moment to look up, closed her eyes and enjoyed the moment. The rainwater felt clean and pure as it poured down against her forehead, cheeks and shaved head. The side of her neck stung as the rain entered a small cut she hadn't even realised she had. The young woman quickly considered any other wounds she might have had beneath her uniform, which she hadn't removed since she'd first pulled it on.

Red had a small first aid box in her rucksack that she could use to tend to any wounds, but she decided to wait. Instead she opened her flask which she'd managed to almost empty, despite being sparing with her consumption of water. She downed the rest of the bottle, fixed it into the dirt, which was quickly turning into mud and allowed it to be filled up with the rainwater. The rain was coming down even heavier by this point, so the flask filled up within minutes. Red quickly tightened its lid, threw the bottle into her rucksack and continued to open her mouth and drink the water as it poured down.

Red had done this only once in The Shell. Not long after she'd first been transported to the United Underworld. She must have been about ten years old at the time. Artificial rain had been spraying down onto the crops and civilians for most of the day. Red had escaped her orphanage and was playing on the streets. She was sitting on the dusty road when she realised that she was thirsty. Looking up, she'd opened her mouth and allowed the water to flood in.

She had sat drinking the water for at least five minutes before she realised that her head had started to pound. Her vision had grown blurry and she felt physically sick. Moments later, she was retching on the road. When the minders from her orphanage had found her, Red was passed out in a pool of her own vomit on the side of the pavement. Her punishment had been receiving a curfew, after her minders decided the young girl must have been drinking alcohol. When Red had explained she'd simply been drinking rainwater, no one believed her.

This had been one of the many things that had led Red to distrust the government. She decided at this young age that the rainwater must have been filled with chemicals. A notion Marcus had always shared with the young activist. The pair believed that this was one of the causes of her elderly friend's raspy cough. And, in Red's eyes, what led to his eventual death. So the fact that Red was standing in the Overworld allowing the rain to fill her mouth, realising that she was unaffected, filled her heart with joy. Like she was being purified with holy water. Like her bionic soul was being cleansed and brought back to life.

As the rain began to ease and finally stop, Red started to walk again. But as she did, she felt a churning feeling in her stomach. She fell to her knees and began to vomit all over the ground. Thick chunks sprayed across the soil, which she realised must have been the squirrel. She could have done with keeping that down.

When Red finally stopped retching, she took a swig from her flask and pressed her hand against her pounding head. What was wrong with her? It was just like the memory she'd been reminded of when she first drank rainwater. Surely the government hadn't managed to poison the clouds in the New Overworld too? She decided it must have been the squirrel disagreeing with her. It had been a very long time since she'd eaten meat. *And who knows what germs it could have been carrying*, she thought to herself.

Once she was certain that she had her gag reflex under control, she climbed back onto her feet and continued walking through the woodland. This time, she picked up the pace and didn't stop to rest or look back.

* * *

Ethan swallowed a large mouthful of the roasted chicken and vegetables that were placed in front of him. At this point in time, eating was the last thing on the young therapist's mind but he was trying to act as normal as possible during his important lunch meeting at the Docklands. Eric Vineyard, a close ally to Ivan Spencer, sat and listened intently to every one of Ethan's words with a stern look on his face. This was nothing out of the ordinary for the government official, seeing as his face appeared to constantly have a hard-nosed expression painted across it.

Eric was a tough looking man, but in a different way to Ivan Spencer. He was far larger than the president, both in height and muscle. His fair hair was shaved, perhaps to align with the therapists who worked for him. Or perhaps just to make him look even tougher. His eyes were a faded shade of grey. He must have been somewhere in his mid to late forties. He had a scar running down the right side of his face, although no one knew where it had come from. Nobody dared to ask.

Dressed in his clinical government attire, Eric interrupted his employee by spitting chewed up chicken, broccoli and gravy out across his chest and back onto this plate.

"Absolutely not. What are you thinking?" he asked, genuinely startled.

Ethan continued what he was saying, speeding up the pace of his words. "It's just, things with Red are taking a little longer than I'd anticipated. She's resilient. And constantly suspicious of us. I feel that if I could just go up and have a look at the fantastic developments in the New Overworld we keep hearing about, it would really give her some hope. Perhaps change the way she sees the government, you know? I could take some pictures, maybe even—"

Eric cut Ethan off before he could continue his explanation. "The answer's no, Ethan. Absolutely not. You of all people should know that it's against government policy for anyone aside from Authorities and high-ranking government officials to visit the New Overworld."

Ethan became agitated as he realised that his idea wasn't going to work. "I know, sir. And I do understand and respect that policy. It's just, as a therapist I thought I might be—"

"You thought you might be what?" Eric interrupted Ethan again, this time becoming visibly annoyed and impatient. His tone became aggressive as he started to hiss out sharp sentences. "You thought you might be exempt from the rule? So what... we start allowing therapists above the ground, then what next? Paramedics? Reactor workers? Hell, why don't we just let every darn civilian of The Shell up there and throw a big party, shall we?"

"No, I'm sorry. I didn't..." Ethan paused as he realised that he didn't know what he was trying to say anymore.

"You didn't think," Eric finished the troubled therapist's sentence for him. "No. You didn't!" Abruptly raising his voice, Eric stood up and sent both of their plates flying towards the floor. A loud crashing sound urged the few other government officials who were in the restaurant to look over. The waiter stood behind the counter, terrified.

"Your job, my boy, is to get into that defiant girl's head

and change her mind about the government," Eric continued. "Okay? So do whatever you have to do. Trick her, drug her or screw her brains out. I don't care. Just finish your damn mission, or I'll finish you!"

Eric began to storm out of the restaurant before turning round and saying: "I'll give you one year. By this time next year, I want to be introduced to whatever-her-name-is as an entirely new woman. You and I will be meeting on a weekly basis, Ethan, so you can keep me updated with how she's doing." With that, Eric left the restaurant, slamming the door behind him.

Ethan took a deep breath and tried to get his thoughts together. Had that really just happened? Had Eric implied that he suspected, or even knew, about Ethan's relationship with his patient? Whatever their relationship was. *The kind that leaves me drugged and gagged*, Ethan thought to himself as he helped the waiter pick the plates up off the floor. The other government officials in the restaurant turned back to their lunches, whispering quietly.

Ethan left the restaurant and headed for his pod. What was he going to do? A meeting on a weekly basis? Eric would get quite a shock at their first scheduled meeting when Ethan didn't turn up. The confused therapist began to wish he'd just stuck with the original plan and waited for the Authority to come back with his uniform. He'd drawn attention to himself. "How did I ever think that would be a good idea?" Ethan muttered out loud to himself as he climbed into his pod.

He closed his eyes for a moment and thought about his missing patient. *Would she even still be alive right now? Is it worth risking my life for someone who might already be dead?* Ethan reopened his eyes and answered his own questions in his head.

Red's not just someone. Of course it's worth it.

Ethan shot off back in the direction of his home to wait for the mystery Authority to arrive. He would continue with the original plan, despite what Eric Vineyard said.

* * *

While the determined therapist sped across the winding pod tracks in The Shell, his even more determined patient continued to walk across the forest miles away on land. Woodland that neither him nor her would have ever imagined to still be living and growing above them. Woodland that housed so much wildlife, from insects and reptiles to birds and rodents. But so far no sign of human life, aside from one fearless woman donning a battered Authority uniform.

It was afternoon when Red finally saw the tall buildings appearing over the trees in the distance. It was still hard to figure out how far away the structures were, but she'd got much closer as they appeared a lot bigger than they had when she originally washed up on the shore. She stopped in her tracks for a moment to look up at the towering structures.

She also hadn't noticed previously how colourful the buildings were. Marbled columns complemented smooth walls in chalky hues, from blues and greens to yellows and pinks. There was something very intricate and beautiful about the structures. Some had dome-shaped tops that were tipped with gold. Some were thick and small, while others were very tall and thin.

It was a city made up of palaces, like the ones Red had read about in the history books Marcus had lent her. In particular, the designs of the buildings reminded her of the grand buildings she'd seen in photographs of ancient India. Like a wider, futuristic version of the Taj Mahal.

But there was no time to stand around gawping at the sight any longer. Red had to keep moving. She had to find out the truth about what was really going on in the New Overworld. As she continued walking, she winced at the thought of Ivan Spencer and his regime living in some beautiful metropolis above the ground while she and the rest of The Shell's residents lived in darkness below the ocean. Why had he done this?

I mean, I knew the guy was twisted, she thought to herself, pushing past twigs and bushes, *but this is just…*

"Inhumane," Red finished the sentence out loud as she spotted something up ahead that made her stop in her tracks. A building, much closer than the palatial ones in the distance and much less tall, but wider. And in stark contrast to the distant Utopia's colourful shades, the building in front of her was a slate grey colour and made from concrete.

In fact, it wasn't a building at all. It was a wall. One that stretched right through the woodland where several trees had obviously been chopped down. On top of the wall was barbed wire, glowing with an electric hum.

Whatever's being kept in there doesn't have much chance of escaping, Red thought to herself, being instantly reminded of The Shell. *Must be for cattle, Ivan Spencer's dinner supply probably.*

At least that was what she thought until she heard the scream.

THIRTEEN

Red's blood turned cold. It had definitely been a human scream. A woman's scream. In fact, it had been more of an agonising shriek. Before she even had the time to process what she was doing, Red began to pace quickly towards the wall. She didn't care if she was in danger. She had to find out what was going on behind it.

Once Red reached the wall, she began to jog beside it. She desperately tried to find a gap in the thick concrete to see what it was hiding. She could hear voices, a low murmuring sound coming from men, but she couldn't make out what they were saying. The wall was far too high to climb. And even if she'd managed to climb it, there was no way she would have made it over the barbed wire alive.

Red felt like calling out over the wall, but common sense stopped her. What good would it have done? If the government were to find out that she was there, they would come and reduce her to a similar shriek. She decided to be more astute, hang back to suss out her environment a bit better, and come up with a plan of action. Although, what good would she be anyway? Charging in with her one raygun and taser. It dawned on Red how little she'd thought the entire thing through.

But she wasn't left wondering for long. As soon as Red turned around, she was met by two Authorities standing side by side with their rayguns pointing towards her.

"Halt! Tell us your ID number, sir," one of the two men spat at her. Red remembered she was dressed in an Authority uniform and was wearing her helmet. They hadn't figured out she was a woman yet. Red stood frozen, keeping her mouth shut.

"Tell us your ID number!" the other Authority spoke even louder, already irritated. Red realised she must have looked rather strange, her uniform battered and broken from her journey so far. They obviously knew something wasn't right. She also realised in this moment that she couldn't remain silent forever. If she dared, they would probably kill her right there on the spot. So, in a moment of madness, Red spoke in the lowest voice she could muster. Trying her best to sound like a gravelly-voiced male.

"I-I'm sorry sir," she said. "I've forgotten it." One of the two Authorities fired his gun, sending a bolt of light shooting towards her. Red felt her entire body fill with sharp electric charge before she fell to the floor and passed out cold.

* * *

The hours Ethan spent waiting for his Authority accomplice to arrive felt like a lifetime. So many scenarios and outcomes were spiralling through his mind. If Red was somehow miraculously still alive, where was she? What was she doing? Was she planning to come back and help the residents of The Shell?

After Eric Vineyard's outburst, Ethan had lost any faith he had left in Ivan Spencer and his regime. He needed to find out the truth about the New Overworld.

His suspicion was that the government had progressed far further with developments than they were letting on. And whether or not the earth above was still a toxic wasteland. He imagined separate cities being built, perhaps in domes above the ground, somewhat like The Shell.

Finally, the doorbell rang. Ethan ran to let the Authority in, before quickly checking outside his doorway to ensure no one in his flat had seen his mysterious guest arrive. They hadn't. Ethan slammed the door.

"I kept my word," said Kyan blankly.

"Not your original promise," Ethan answered sternly. "You're not helping me gain much trust in you."

Kyan paced the room before taking a seat. Then, much to Ethan's surprise, he removed his helmet.

Ethan didn't recognise Kyan. Why would he? Kyan spent his life behind the camera, not in front of it. But the very fact that he was willing to reveal his identity was enough to make Ethan feel reassured. That was a big commitment.

"Look, Ethan. If we're going to even try to rescue your patient, you're going to have to start by trusting me. My name is Kyan and I'm the mind behind Shareflow."

Ethan looked confused. "The whistleblowing website?" he asked, unable to disguise his shock. Ethan was aware of the website, but he'd never paid much attention to it.

"Yes. I also work as a producer at the United Underworld Studios, editing footage of Ivan Spencer's lies," he continued. "So now you understand what I'm sacrificing here."

After a few moments, once the news had been fully absorbed, Ethan did understand.

"I'm sorry, Kyan," he said. "I obviously had no idea." Kyan smiled.

"It's ok, brother. Why would you?" he asked reassuringly. "At least now you know how I've been risking my life every day. So if your girl's willing to take a risk this big, why wouldn't I risk my life too? I've decided to devote my life to uncovering the lies our government is feeding us. And if it means dying for that cause… well, so be it."

Now it was Ethan that was smiling. "Then let's do this."

There was a moment's silence as it dawned on the two men that they had finally properly met. Their mission all at once felt so much more achievable. And so much more risky, considering the circumstances. Kyan ran his hand through his shaved mohawk before heading over to retrieve the extra uniform from his bag. As he did, Ethan began to explain his meeting with Eric Vineyard.

"So obviously it's a real concern, but there's nothing I can do. Like you said, it's a risk I'm just going to have to take."

Kyan froze, before throwing the uniform back into his bag. Ethan looked confused.

"What's the problem?" he asked.

"Brother, haven't you just been listening to what you're saying?" Kyan's voice was raised and his tone had changed. "They're onto you. Which means if you come with me, they'll come looking for us much quicker!"

This time it was Ethan's turn to look confused. "I think there's just as much chance that they'll come looking for you when Spencer's team notices you haven't turned up at work," said Ethan, visibly annoyed.

"Of course they will. Which is why I'm leaving a suicide note," Kyan replied.

Ethan looked stunned. "A suicide note? But there'll be no body?"

Kyan pulled out a cigarette from his top pocket.

"Mind if I smoke?" he asked.

Ethan rolled his eyes. "Be my guest."

Kyan sparked his lighter and paused for a moment as he watched the tip of the cigarette burn.

"They'll find what's supposedly left of me in the Incinerator." The hairs on the back of Ethan's neck stood up.

"You mean—"

"That's right, brother," Kyan interrupted. "As far as the old dog's concerned, I'm going into the ashes."

The Incinerator was an enormous furnace located in the east of The Shell, attached to part of the Reactor. It was used to burn down the United Underworld's waste into ash.

Suicide rates were unsurprisingly high in The Shell, with many people deciding they would rather die than continue their dismal day-to-day existence. The government didn't acknowledge this depressing truth, let alone do anything to try and stop it.

The Incinerator was where many people would head when they decided to end their lives. They would climb up a ladder into the easily-accessible furnace, plunge in and burn themselves to smithereens. This horrific suicidal method was nicknamed *going into the ashes* and was a very well-known way to escape the bleakness of The Shell.

Ethan gulped down some air as he spared a thought to whatever it could be Kyan was planning to cremate.

"Then I'll do the same," he said finally.

"What? Are you stupid? That'll be way too suspicious, we'll end up both getting killed," said Kyan. "No, I've made up my mind. I'm going up to find her, you're staying down here and acting like everything's normal."

"No way," Ethan responded, shaking his head. "No way am I staying down here when I know Red's in danger."

Kyan got up and took the uniform back out of the bag.

"Look, brother. It's not about playing the hero here. You and I both know our chances are slim up there, but there's no point us both getting killed when there's still a chance of Red's life being saved." Kyan handed Ethan the uniform. "Here, you can still have this. It's ultimately your decision if you want to risk both our lives and come play superman, so I'm not going to keep this from you. But what I'm saying is – give it some thought. Be smart."

Ethan looked down at the uniform and considered his options, few as they were. Kyan got up and spoke again. "I say I head up there, see what I find. We'll keep in touch through our connectors if we can. If not, I'll message you if I can get access to the internet. And keep an eye on Shareflow, obviously." He started to walk towards the door.

"Wait... so, you're just going to go now?" Ethan looked surprised.

"Well, what would you rather: we sit around and talk about it all night? That's another night Red's up there somewhere on her own." Kyan reached out and put his hand on Ethan's shoulder. "Do the right thing, brother. Play your part. Keep Eric what's-his-face distracted. I'm gonna bring back your girl."

The pain felt like a dagger through Ethan's chest as he realised Kyan's plan was the right thing to do. How he was actually going to stay put and keep quiet was an entirely different matter. It would be nothing less than torture.

"If I don't hear from you in the next twenty-four hours, I'm coming straight up," Ethan said, grasping the mask of the uniform in his hands.

"You'll hear from me," Kyan replied reassuringly.

How wrong he was.

FOURTEEN

The air smelt like smouldering soot and stagnant water. Red opened her striking yet bloodshot green eyes slowly as she regained consciousness. At first, her vision was blurry. When she started to regain focus, she realised that she was lying down on what felt like cold concrete. Darkness surrounded her.

As she tried to lift up her arms, she realised that they were strapped down with what felt like leather clasps. The same with her feet. She screamed.

In less than ten seconds someone appeared in the room.

"Be quiet, you stupid animal!" shouted a woman's voice. Harsh artificial light lit up the room and standing directly above Red was someone she instantly recognised. It was Ivan Spencer's daughter, Carmen.

Her emaciated face made her look similar to her father, but she was still somehow strangely beautiful. Her hair was currently dyed a mixture of yellow and green. Her eyes a greyish blue, further mirroring her father's appearance.

"You," whispered Red. It was all she could muster through her confusion. Carmen ignored her response and walked towards the other side of the room.

"Really I should just kill you right now, it would be far easier," she said bluntly. "Trying to escape The Plant is obviously an instant ticket to death." Red was confused. *The Plant? Surely she meant to say The Shell*, she wondered to herself. *Unless they have a different name for it up here.*

"But all in good time. You still have your purpose right now, obviously," Carmen continued. "I'm sure daddy wouldn't be pleased if I murdered another one of his cattle too early."

Now Red was beyond confusion. What did she mean, *cattle*? She noticed another man in the room. Tall, broad and extremely pasty, the man's face was worn and he was dressed all in black. His eyes were sunken back into their sockets. He was quite hideous.

"Throw her back in with the other animals," said Carmen as she walked out of the room. The tall man unfastened the buckles on Red's arms and pulled her upright. Her body felt sore from the shock of the raygun she'd been stunned with. She couldn't believe she was still alive.

The man tied Red's arms behind her back as she tried to struggle. She felt too weak to put up a fight. Not to mention the man was extremely broad and stocky. There was no way she could escape his grasp. He began to lead her down a long corridor.

Red realised that she was no longer in the Authority uniform, unsurprisingly. Instead she was clothed in an androgynous loose-fitting ensemble that had both a long-sleeved top half and trousers. The uniform was a slate-grey colour, similar to what Reactor workers in The Shell wore. She was barefoot.

The whispering was the first thing Red noticed as she was being dragged along the thin, dark corridor in front of her. Coming from both sides, like ghosts in the night. Metallic door after metallic door was passed, with a small window on the top of each one that featured metal bars. She tried to peek into one but as she did her arm was tightened harder behind her back.

Red didn't even have the strength to scream. She felt so weak from the raygun's shock that she decided to just keep walking. Then, she heard more piercing shrieks. Just like the one she'd heard outside, female screams were coming from both sides of her. Red's heart dropped to her stomach as she considered her fate.

The tall man dragged Red down a few more corridors, before he finally stopped. He opened a door on the right and threw the young woman in. She fell on the cold, hard floor with a thud, and he slammed the door.

After a few seconds of silence, Red heard a quiet voice across the room.

"Are you all right, lady?" the female voice whispered. Red slowly picked herself upright and turned around to face the stranger. Staring back at her was a woman who looked like she was in her late twenties. She had an olive skin tone, but Red couldn't make out the colour of her eyes in the dark room. She was in the same grey uniform that Red was wearing and was also barefoot. But most shockingly of all, her head was shaved. Just like Red's.

"Your hair—" Red croaked, "your hair's shaved too?"

The woman looked stunned. "Well of course it is, honey. Have you gone nuts?" she asked. "We've all got skin'eds in 'ere."

Red's eyes darted around the room trying to familiarise herself with her new surroundings. The space was dark, but she could just about make out the concrete walls. Grime ran down them where there were no windows to let the damp air ventilate. The small gap at the top of the thick steel door let in a tiny bit of light through its bars.

"Who are you?" the woman asked, looking genuinely mystified. So many thoughts were racing through Red's head. Could she trust this woman? Could she trust anyone she met? She soon realised her choices were pretty limited if she was going to start actually finding out any answers.

"My name's Red," she said slowly.

The stranger's face eased a little when she realised her new roommate was actually going to start letting her in.

"I'm Trip. Nice to meet you." She extended her hand out.

Red stared at it for a moment, before she hesitantly held her hand up to be shaken.

"Don't worry, I'm not gonna hurt you, Red," said Trip, genuinely. "I'm not one of 'em." She pointed towards the door, or at least to the people behind it.

Trip turned her attention back to Red.

"You're not from in 'ere, are you?" Her eyes narrowed as if she was trying to read Red's mind. Red stayed silent, but shook her head. Trip's eyes widened.

"You mean, you're from outside?" she asked bewilderedly.

This time it was Red's turn to look confused. "I mean... from down there!" She pointed towards the ground.

This time Trip's eyes almost popped out of their sockets. "The Shell?" She tried to whisper but couldn't contain her shock and what sounded like excitement.

Red nodded, once again. "You mean, you're not?" she asked, also feeling excitement bubbling from within her. If this was the case, it was the first proper conversation she'd had with someone from outside of The Shell in over a decade.

Trip shook her head. "No honey, I'm not. I wish I was. And once I've filled you in on a few things you're gonna wish you were back down there too."

Red felt her heart sink to her stomach. She hadn't thought it would be physically possible for anyone to convince her she'd rather be back down in the dismal world she'd fought so hard to escape.

"But before we get to all that, I've jus' gotta tell you one thing," Trip said quickly. "Whatever 'appens, we can't let 'em find out you're from down there. I 'ave no idea how you escaped, honey. And you're lucky Carmen didn't realise you ain't one of us. Because if they find out..." Trip stopped her sentence there. There was no need for her to explain any more. Red got the idea.

"There's so much I need to ask you," Red began, sensing that Trip was someone she could trust. Besides, she realised her options were restricted if she didn't.

"I mean, if you're not from The Shell... then where are you from?" All of a sudden, a loud pounding could be heard on the cell's door.

"Be quiet in there!" the man's voice was loud and aggressive. Trip shook her head and held her finger to Red's lips gently. "Not now," she whispered. "Let's talk tomorrow."

With that, Red lay down on a few rags that had been left to sleep on and readied herself for what would undoubtedly be another sleepless night. Although as terrified and confused as she was, she also felt anticipation to finally be getting closer to some answers. To finally getting closer to uncovering the truth.

* * *

As night fell across The Shell and the artificial lights went out, Kyan knew this was his greatest chance of trying to escape. His plan was the same as Red's had been, but he was going to risk staying aboard the vessel as it docked at the Overworld. He planned to then follow the other Authorities through the front exit.

Kyan's advantage was not only that he was male, which gave him a better chance of posing as an Authority, but that he had a vast knowledge of how Authorities behaved and interacted. His years of working in the United Underworld Studios had allowed him to watch and observe the blunt and aggressive men up close and personal. All of this had been research leading the young rebel to this moment. The moment he was going to attempt to finally escape The Shell.

Kyan moved quickly from his pod to where a small group of Authorities were beginning to form outside the exit docks of the United Underworld. He knew that vessels were sent up to the Overworld each night carrying large amounts of cargo. Despite these vessels being computer-operated, they always needed to be accompanied by Authorities.

Kyan managed to sneak himself between the other gormless drones, clothed in the same clinical-white uniform, without being noticed. He knew he would need to remain confident if he even stood a chance of blending in with them. Kyan marched in unison with the Authorities as they began to board the vessel. He listened in to a conversation two of the masked men were having.

"It'll happen when the time's right, Vex. You jus' need to be patient."

"Yeah I know, I know. I jus' feel like we've bin waitin' long enough now, you know? I'm ready to be up there for good. No more of this crawlin' around down 'ere like sewer rats."

It dawned on Kyan how the Authorities were just as eager to live back above the ground as civilians were. He thought to himself how Ivan Spencer was probably feeding them the same lies he told everyone else.

Kyan kept quiet as the vessel jolted a few times when it started up, before quickly pushing forward and upwards as it headed towards the surface. He took a deep breath and said a short prayer in his head. He wasn't a religious man, but if there were a god – he'd be needing them.

Kyan wasn't the only Authority standing in silence, which worked in his favour. Most of the other men were doing the same thing, apart from a few who spoke quietly. Laughing at each other's jokes. Kyan could feel his stomach churning. Not only at the thought of getting caught, but at what could have been waiting for him in the Overworld.

After what felt like a lifetime, the vessel carrying sixteen

Authorities and one terrified imposter, reached its final destination. The men started to march forward, with Kyan mimicking their exact movements.

As he walked, his eyes darted around through his tinted dome-shaped helmet. Taking in his surroundings. The men had left behind the vessel at the arrival bay and were walking through a claustrophobic corridor. Much like the entrance to The Shell. The Authority uniforms blended in with the bleak whiteness of the walls.

Finally, a dark starry sky could be seen as the men reached the end of the corridor. Kyan took another deep breath and stepped outside into the Overworld. He could not believe his eyes.

Standing before him was a beautiful skyline made up of glowing palatial buildings. The New Overworld, which Kyan had been led to believe was hardly in the early stages of development, stood looking more complete than London ever had.

But more surprising to Kyan was what he had often pondered but never thought would actually be true. The same thing Red had discovered herself a mere twenty-four hours prior. The world stood unharmed from the asteroid that Ivan Spencer had led everyone to believe had plummeted towards the planet.

Kyan felt a burning inside of him that he knew needed to be controlled. He continued to follow the Authorities towards the Utopia in front of him, with a fingernail moon hanging in the sky above. Where their final destination was, he had no idea. All he knew was that if he didn't find a way to slip away from the Authorities soon, he would be in danger. Serious danger.

Once the group of masked men reached the entrance to the city, an enormous gate that ran as far as the eye could make out greeted them. It was tall, but this didn't stop Kyan from being able to see all the tops of the city's buildings.

One of the men spoke into a speaker at the gate's door. "We're here with the N45 cargo," he said abruptly. The door opened slowly, revealing the entrance to the shiny new world.

Once again, Kyan couldn't believe his eyes. It was like he was staring into an oil painting. Into a world even more beautiful than the one he remembered. The dismal reality of The Shell beneath seemed like a distant nightmare compared to the paradise in front of him.

The buildings were laced with gold. The streets were cleaner than the hallways of a palace. Palm trees that were all the same size stood side by side lining the street's marble pavements. Out of all the bizarre things Kyan was absorbing, seeing such lush palm trees in England was one of the most bewildering.

A line of Authorities stood behind the gate, but they looked different to the men standing beside him. Their uniform was similar, but had a soft lilac hue with silver detailing. Kyan couldn't believe how obvious the division was. The hierarchy. Surely it wouldn't be too hard to convince the lower Authorities to join forces with citizens of The Shell and revolt?

The thought of revolution was the only thing that kept Kyan going at this point. He'd wanted to see justice occur for so long and at this stage it seemed closer than ever. All he had to do was find a way to get the message down to the people of The Shell. Inform them of the lies they had been fed. Surely if they saw this with their own eyes it would be enough to convince them to fight back? He had to believe they would, despite everything they had ignored on Shareflow already.

One of the New Overworld's *High* Authorities began talking to an Authority from The Shell, who was standing too far away from Kyan for him to hear what was being said. The Authority then removed his glove and held his hand up to be scanned by a piece of machinery the High Authority was holding. It made a sound of approval, before the Authority was allowed to proceed forward.

Kyan's heart sunk to his gut. Fingerprint detection. How had he not even considered this? As if it would have been that easy! As if he could have just snuck into the Overworld simply because he had access to an Authority's uniform. Kyan knew at this point there was no way Red could have even survived trying to escape, let alone enter the New Overworld.

He thought in that moment how awful it must have been for Red. She'd been the first person to be proven right about her distrust of the government and its corruption. She would no doubt have been made to suffer for it.

But Kyan couldn't stand around pondering for long. The High Authority was quickly working his way through the Authorities next to him. One by one approving their fingerprints and allowing them to enter the dream-like city. Kyan knew this was it. The end of the line. His moment to change the future. If he was ever going to.

Slowly and subtly, Kyan reached for his connector in the

side of his boot. He kept his eyes on the men around him, who were waiting patiently to be allowed in the gate and thankfully not paying any attention to him. Kyan shot his glance down to the device. To his amazement, he realised that he still had a connection. He was able to access the backend of Shareflow.

This was his chance. Kyan quickly took a picture of the glistening city and began tapping words into the post in capital letters:

MY NAME IS KYAN EISENBERG AND I AM IN THE NEW OVERWORLD. I SNUCK UP HERE TO BE GREETED BY AN UNTOUCHED WORLD. THE ASTEROID WAS ALL A LIE FED TO US BY THE GOVERNMENT. THERE IS A BEAUTIFUL CITY UP HERE LACED WITH GOLD. WHEN YOU READ THIS I WILL PROBABLY BE DEAD BUT YOU MUST BELIEVE ME AND YOU MUST ACT NOW! THE TIME HAS COME TO REVOLT!

"Hey, what are you doing?" one of the Authorities beside Kyan had noticed him.

Kyan quickly tapped a button that set his leak live.

"Get him!" one of the men in front called out. Two of the men beside Kyan grabbed him and threw his connector out of his hand and onto the floor, where it smashed into pieces.

That's done me a favour, Kyan thought as he realised Ivan Spencer wouldn't be able to hack into Shareflow and delete his message.

The two men brought Kyan before the High Authority holding the fingerprint detector and pulled off his glove. Kyan willingly held his hand up towards the device before it let out a shrill sound, indicating his identity hadn't been approved.

"Arrest him!" the High Authority yelled. Two of the High Authorities forcefully tied Kyan's arms together and dragged him towards the city. It didn't feel much like a paradise anymore.

FIFTEEN

Red must have only slept for a few hours in total. Even so, it was the best sleep she'd had in days, which actually made her feel worse. Her body had begun trying to repair itself from all the sleep she'd lost. Not to mention the fact that she could feel all the cuts and bruises she'd acquired throughout her journey as they throbbed across her body.

As she got up, Red felt a dull ache in her back where she'd been sleeping on the concrete floor. She realised it'd been more comfortable sleeping under the tree in the forest.

"Rise and shine, sleepyhead." Trip was sat upright, filing her nails. Red could see her much clearer as it was daytime and bright light flooded into the cell. Her face was worn, with a large birthmark across her left cheek. Her eyes were a dullish grey, as if they'd once been blue but the life had been drained out of them.

Despite all this, Trip's face had a warmness that led Red

to feel like she could be at ease with her. *Perhaps it's women's intuition*, Red thought to herself as she smoothed her hand over her shaved head and rubbed her eyes.

"How long was I out?" she asked, realising she literally had no idea.

"Not long enough. But they'll be along in a minute bangin' on the door," Trip replied. "So at least this gives us a few more minutes to talk."

There was so much Red wanted to ask her new accomplice. She didn't even know where to begin. "Where did you come from?" she asked plainly.

Trip got up and moved towards Red, before sitting down right beside her. When she spoke, she spoke quickly and in whispers:

"Ok. We don't 'ave much time so I'll only say this once and won't be able to go into too much detail. As you've probably already gathered, there was no asteroid. The whole thing was a lie. A fix. Set up to banish humanity down t'The Shell and start again. The world was gettin' too overpopulated and Spencer wanted to focus on creatin' a new race.

"I was part of the big group that was kept above the ground to help start this new population. We're all women 'ere, made pregnant through artificial insem'nation. We give birth, our babies are taken away and then the same thing 'appens again. If we lose our fertility or if it takes too long to impregnate us, we're slaughtered like cattle. That's why you heard the screams."

At this point, Red stopped listening. Not intentionally, she just couldn't hear anymore. Trip's words started to fade away into a sort of static white noise as the blood rushed to Red's brain. There was only one thing she could think of. One thing that pulsed through her body like a drug.

The thought that her mother, who had been in the group left behind in the Overworld, could still be alive.

The idea sent so much adrenaline rushing through Red's veins that it felt like an electric shock. She began to physically tremble. Even her rage towards Ivan Spencer and his regime was surpassed by the feeling of elation that her mother could still be living and breathing up in the New Overworld somewhere. And perhaps she even had half-brothers and sisters!

Red quickly tuned back into what Trip was saying:

"Which is why you're so lucky you 'ave a shaved 'ead and Carmen didn't recognise you as an outsider from The Plant. We all 'ave that up 'ere, do you all 'ave it down there too then?"

Before Red even had a chance to answer, another thought dawned on her. "I'm not pregnant." No sooner had the three simple words been quietly muttered, a loud bang on the door made both women jolt.

Trip shook her head and looked sympathetic.

"I'm so sorry, Red."

The door swung open and two men dressed all in white entered to escort the women out into the hallway. Red wanted to ask Trip where they were going, but knew this would be a mistake. She was just going to have to follow suit.

As she walked in silence, Red realised that everything around her was hazy, like she was in a dream. But she knew the dream would soon be turned into a nightmare when she was found out to be an intruder. She feared it could happen right in front of her mother's eyes.

The two women were guided down the long corridor following a string of several other women. Red was glad Trip had managed to warn her of the situation, because if she hadn't, she would have had a huge shock once they had left their cell.

As Red followed the line of women in front of her, she could make out how they all resembled one another. Not only through their shaved heads that were all kept at the same length. Not simply through their pregnant stomachs, all showing they were at different phases in their pregnancies. But because of their worn-down faces. Faces that were filled with sadness. And fear.

While Red was guided further and further down the corridor past the cells, the fact that Trip was right behind her comforted her in a strange way. Even though she had no idea what she was walking towards, Trip's presence made her feel safe.

Or perhaps it was the thought of her mother being alive. She'd always felt like she was out there somewhere, watching over her like an angel. Maybe this was what all the dreams had signified? Like they had been premonitions. Or signals from her mother in the Overworld. Telling her everything was going to be all right.

Red's daydream was interrupted by the screams coming from the room on the left-hand side of her. Deafening shrieks that pierced through the air like scissors cutting through cloth. She couldn't help but turn around to look at Trip, who shot her a quick glance that said: "Turn back around." Red listened to her new friend's eyes.

Before long, Red realised that one by one the women were

being led into a room and returned after a minute or so. Most of them were ushered through a door on the right, but once in a while a woman was reluctantly pulled into the room on the left, which was where the screams were coming from. Red swallowed hard when she realised what was happening.

The women were having their babies checked. It was obviously a quick scan, nothing too detailed. But enough to figure out whether the baby was healthy enough. *Or*, Red gulped, *whether it even exists!*

She could feel the fear bubbling within her as she stepped closer and closer to the door. This was it. There was no going back. Nowhere to run. How ironic that her longing to escape The Shell had led her to this. Something so much worse. At least the women in The Shell had the opportunity to work as cleaners at the Reactor. This was beyond sexism. This was inhumane.

The fear Red felt was quickly replaced by rage towards Ivan Spencer. As if she didn't hate him enough already. Although this time she felt he'd surpassed even himself with cruelty. Just when she didn't think it was possible for the dictator to surprise her, Red found herself feeling truly horrified as she stood in line at the pregnancy plant.

She considered what would happen to her once they found out that she was not carrying a child. She could only imagine the grim torture she would face when put in front of Ivan Spencer. Or perhaps she wouldn't even make it that far. She was certain Carmen would put an end to her pretty swiftly once she realised Red had managed to pose as a prisoner.

It was Red's turn to enter the room. Her vision quickly came back into focus as she realised that two men were guiding her into a small dimly-lit room. To her surprise, an elderly woman stood in the room holding a small electronic device. Her silver hair was scraped back exposing her wrinkled face. She must have been at least eighty years old.

Red considered her options. She could try and run, although she knew she wouldn't even make it out of the room alive. She could just save the old woman the trouble and tell her straight up that she wasn't going to find anything inside her stomach besides the butterflies that were frantically flapping around, crashing into one another.

She decided she'd do none of the above. She would just let the zombies discover for themselves before leading her to her fate.

One of the two men grabbed Red by her arm and pulled her over to where the old woman was standing. In the blink of an eye she held the device up to Red's stomach where it made a quick beeping sound. Up on a screen next to the two women flashed the words FERTILISATION SUCCESSFUL.

"All fine. Next," the elderly woman said flatly. Red couldn't believe her eyes or ears.

The two men led her out of the room and into the room on the right. On her way Red caught sight of Trip's facial expression, which was just as shocked and confused.

Not only was Red a prisoner with a bleak future ahead of her. She was also a prisoner carrying a child.

Ethan's child.

* * *

Ethan swiftly opened his eyes and reached straight for his

connector. Still nothing. He'd waited up most of the night to hear from Kyan but feared the device wouldn't work in the Overworld.

A cold shiver ran down the therapist's back as he considered his limited options. By this point, both Red and Kyan were lost somewhere above the ground. Most probably dead. He knew he couldn't wait around much longer twiddling his thumbs.

For what it was worth, Ethan decided to check Shareflow next. Just in case. What else could he have done? As soon as the website loaded up on his connector's screen, nothing could have prepared him for what he was about to see. The shiver that was running up and down his spine turned even colder.

Kyan's frantic words, typed out in capital letters to emphasise their importance and immediacy, glared back at Ethan like hawks circling their prey. A grainy, out of focus picture of what appeared to be a cityscape accompanied the message. He read the leak again at least five times before it finally began to sink in.

The asteroid was a lie. The world was untouched. His sister could be alive. Red could be alive.

These final realisations were what pushed Ethan to climb straight out of bed and head over to Delta's. Could she already know?

As Ethan began to glide through The Shell in his pod, he thought to himself how he must be one of the only people to have already read the news. Although the streets of the United Underworld always looked weathered and abandoned, he was certain they would start looking even worse once people realised how much they had been duped.

He envisioned the Armageddon that could follow and felt a sudden burst of excitement in his stomach. Could this lead to what Red had yearned for so long? The people of The Shell finally fighting back against Ivan Spencer and his regime? Would there finally be a revolution?

Ethan parked his pod a few metres away from Delta's level before sprinting inside. He leapt into the rusty old lift that slowly brought him up to Delta's floor, before diving down the corridor and ringing the buzzer to her home.

"Delta! Delta, are you home? It's me, Ethan!" To Ethan's surprise, it was Xavier who opened the door, clutching a black baseball bat in his hands.

"Woah, slow down there!" said Ethan, taking a few steps backwards slowly.

"Stop, Xavier! It's ok," Delta said as she appeared behind her lover. "This is our friend, Ethan. He's with us." Delta grabbed both men by the arms, pulled them inside the flat and slammed the door.

Ethan stood for a moment in shock at the demolition in front of him. Smashed devices, broken glass and even a dent in the wall. He looked round at Xavier who stood in silence, with an enraged look on his face. He then turned to Delta, who he realised had been crying. Red's cat, Aura, was cowering in a corner. Visibly trembling.

"I take it you've both been on Shareflow this morning," Ethan said plainly.

"I've been checking it religiously since you told me that *Authority* was going above the ground," Delta replied, surrounding the word with air quotes. "It only went up a couple of hours ago, I doubt many people know yet. No one ever checks it. I never did before Red left, although she always told me I should." Delta began fighting back her tears.

Xavier swung his baseball bat into the side of the wall causing it to crack slightly. Delta and Ethan jumped with shock. Aura quickly scampered out of the room.

"I can't believe I've been such a fool! Slaving away to the government all these years. For what? To keep the power running up there, I bet," Xavier shouted, pointing his weapon towards the ceiling. He was unable to disguise the frustration in his voice.

"Xavier, I know you're angry. But destroying my home is not helping!" Delta said, grabbing the baseball bat off of her boyfriend.

"I can't believe you've been keeping this from me, didn't you think you could trust me?" Xavier asked.

Ethan realised Delta obviously hadn't told her boyfriend about Red escaping The Shell yet. She'd kept her promise.

"Because I knew you would think she was an idiot," Delta replied. "Don't forget you've been on the government's side up until now. And look how wrong we were about that!"

"Yes, I know," Xavier said. "But you made me believe she was just out there somewhere on the streets of The Shell! I was worried sick."

"You were worried sick?" Delta responded. "Imagine how I felt knowing she's up there somewhere, probably dead—"

At this point Ethan had to interrupt. He had no intention of standing around wasting time in the middle of an argument. Not when there was fresh hope for both Red and his sister,

Leyla, being alive.

"Look guys, I'm just as shocked and confused as you both are," he said abruptly. "But we have to do something. We need to act fast."

This time Xavier turned his focus to Ethan. "And I still can't work out how you supposedly didn't know all this," said Xavier. "You work for the government don't you, surely you had an inkling?"

"Xavier!" Delta interrupted. "Of course he didn't. We work for the government too and we had no idea! Besides, Ethan's in love with Red. So he'd have no reason to have kept that from her. Or anyone for that matter."

Ethan's face turned slightly pink at Delta's statement. Was it really that obvious he had fallen in love with his patient? It was something he hadn't even consciously admitted to himself. But Delta was right. This was love. And he wasn't going to give up trying to save Red until he knew for certain whether she was dead or alive.

"You're right, Ethan," Delta continued. "We do need to act fast. We have to save our girl before it's too late."

The young therapist looked relieved that the argument was over and the attention was finally directed towards making a plan. "Ok, so are we going to go up together or should I go alone?" Ethan asked. "Perhaps you guys should stay down here and act normal."

Delta shook her head. "No, Ethan. Things are different now, the situation's changed," she said blankly before continuing:

"In a matter of hours everybody in The Shell will know

that the asteroid was a lie and will want answers. As soon as they realise they won't be getting any, their confusion will turn to anger. The anger will turn to violence, worse than the United Underworld already knows. It won't take long for the Authorities to tighten up security, particularly as they've obviously already caught Kyan dressed in one of their uniforms. Before we know it, the Authorities will be fighting back."

Ethan nodded in agreement. He knew what Delta was saying was right, as much as he hated to hear it. "So what are we going to do?" he asked.

Delta held the baseball bat up to signal a sign of power and authority. "If we can't go up there, then we need to focus on what we can do down here." Then, much to the surprise of both Ethan and Xavier, Delta defiantly sent the baseball bat crashing through the glass table beside her. Fragments of broken glass were sent crashing to the floor beneath her feet. The room went quiet.

* * *

As her three friends began to devise yet another plan to try and come to her rescue, Red sat in silence in her cell opposite the grimy white brick wall.

She was *pregnant*? Red wasn't sure whether she was more shocked about the fact that she would be having a baby, or how fortunate she was to have avoided being found out by Carmen. She decided the pregnancy itself was definitely what shocked her the most.

Red had never imagined having children. She'd never wanted them. Not because she disliked them as such, she'd just never really been around any since she was a child herself. She'd hated the idea of bringing another human being into such a dismal world. The thought of being born in The Shell, of growing up never knowing what fresh air or natural light felt like, filled her with sadness and fear.

Now that she was actually pregnant with the child of a man she didn't even know if she would ever see again, her fear was so much worse. The vileness of The Shell paled in comparison to The Plant. She had no idea where her child would be taken once they were born. Most probably handed over to Ivan Spencer to grow up in his new world, whatever that was like.

Red had no idea what sort of evil Ivan Spencer was still capable of. Not to mention the cruelty he was putting the women inside The Plant through.

But all of this just made her feel more determined. Determined to escape The Plant and come back for all the other women. Determined to find her mother, who she was certain was alive. Determined to expose the truth to the people of The Shell and help them overturn Ivan Spencer and his regime.

Determined to kill the dictator, who she loathed so greatly, with her own two hands. Determined to be reunited with Ethan once more. To put her arms around him and tell him about their child. Determined to see her child born into a world not dictated by evil. A free world.

How she was going to achieve all of this, she still wasn't quite sure.

SIXTEEN

When Kyan opened his eyes, he realised that he wasn't alone in his chamber. Next to him, only just visible from a slither of bright light cutting through the darkness, was an elderly man stripped down to his underwear. Shackled to the wall. The man's body was so skinny and frail that he looked like a skeleton. The thin layer of skin that only just shielded his bones was covered in cuts and bruises.

As the man lifted his head slowly to reveal two sunken grey eyes, Kyan guessed instantly who it was.

"Professor… Prothero?" he asked, barely managing a whisper. Kyan had no idea how long he had been out cold. He also realised that his own arms were tied above him with chains, attaching him to the grimy, moss-covered wall. His skin stung from wounds that felt fresh. His body throbbed as if it had been brutally beaten.

The old man nodded slowly, looking in serious pain as he

did. Kyan winced at what the government had done to such an elderly man. Someone who had dedicated his life to research and discovery.

"My name's Kyan," he continued. "I'm the person behind Shareflow, who you tried to contact."

A wave of realisation overtook the professor's face. After a brief pause, he opened his mouth to speak. A burst of blood fell out and poured down his chin. He coughed a couple of times before managing to get his words out.

"What I tried to tell you," he croaked, as if it was the first time he'd spoken in a very long time. "Is that they've been putting chemicals in the water. To keep us docile."

As shocking as the scientist's finding was, it seemed like nothing compared to everything Kyan had discovered in the past few hours. The fact that The Shell's artificial raindrops contained drugs was just another nail in a very large coffin the government had built.

Kyan felt a pang of sadness for the old man as he realised he probably didn't even know where he was. He probably didn't even know that the asteroid had been a hoax.

Just as this realisation began to sink in and Kyan opened his mouth to respond, a man entered the room. Kyan swung his head round to be greeted by two Authorities. Standing in between them was Ivan Spencer. The president's personal assistant, Han Eden, followed a few steps behind. Kyan's blood ran colder than ice.

"Hello, Kyan," Ivan Spencer began softly, "what a privilege to finally meet the mastermind behind Shareflow."

Kyan felt his stomach churn as he remembered the leak

he made onto his website, which had revealed his identity. He'd known he was going to die anyway, so he had nothing to lose. His name might as well have gone down in history for something noble.

"Although I guess we've met before really," Ivan Spencer continued, before pausing briefly. "On occasion," he concluded. The leader's tone had turned stern. It was obvious how annoyed he was after being foiled for so long by someone working right under his nose. It was also clear how much he was revelling in having the young man at his mercy. Like a spider stuck under a wine glass.

Kyan decided to speak, for what it was worth. "You won't get away with what you've done. Pretty soon word will get out down there and people will rise up. They'll want answers."

Ivan Spencer scoffed at the rebel's threat. "Oh please, boy," he began. "You give your people too much credit. Do you really think they will actually do anything? People live in fear. They don't want to rock the boat."

"Not everyone's afraid of you," said Kyan, with conviction. Ivan Spencer, who had been pacing the room, stopped dead in his tracks.

"You might be right," he said. "But they should be." With that, he nodded to give signal to one of the Authorities standing next to him. The Authority pulled a small dagger out from the side of his belt buckle. The blade glistened as the thin beam of light penetrating the room reflected against it.

Kyan shook his head.

"You don't need to do this," he began, his voice trembling. Ivan Spencer smiled, although his thin lips revealed no signs of warmth or empathy. "Oh, but I insist," he said sarcastically.

The Authority launched towards Professor Prothero, who let out a weak cry. The man then began to violently saw the back of the old man's neck.

The process of removing Professor Prothero's head was not a quick one. Kyan tried to keep his eyes shut as the gruesome act took place, but the other Authority in the room forced them open. Ivan Spencer and his assistant simply stood in silence and watched the entire act of brutality take place.

Finally, the elderly man was out of his misery as his severed head fell into a pool of blood and rolled across the dirty floor. His body remained upright, his arms still shackled to the walls. Ivan Spencer walked over to the dead scientist's head, bent down and picked it up. He clutched the old man's white hair, using it to lift the decapitated head up directly in front of Kyan's vision.

"Now look what you made me do," Ivan Spencer said, without a glimmer of remorse.

Kyan couldn't contain his fear any longer. "What do you want from me?" he asked, turning his face away from the grotesque scene in front of him. "Tell me what you want, just please don't do that to me!" Kyan couldn't believe what he was saying, but in this moment he would have done anything to avoid such a horrific end to his own life.

Ivan Spencer threw the head to the floor. It cracked as it hit the concrete.

"I want you to give us the login to Shareflow!" he spat in a shrill tone.

Kyan felt the surprise resonate within him. He realised how despite the fact he'd dropped his connector after publishing his leak, which would have instantly ended up in the hands of the Authorities, Ivan Spencer and his regime had still not managed to hack into the website's back-end.

"But it's too late," said Kyan. "What use would that be now?"

Ivan Spencer began pacing the room again. "Not everyone reads your silly little website," he replied. "So I'm sure there's still time to replace what you wrote with something we've written."

Kyan winced at the thought of what that could be, before considering his options. He turned to face what was left of Professor Prothero and realised that his fate had already been decided. Whether he gave the passcode to Ivan Spencer or not, he knew he would end up with his head rolling across the floor. And if his leak had any chance of reaching enough people to begin a revolution, this was a risk he was willing to take. He was ready to die for what he'd fought so hard for.

"No," said Kyan.

Ivan Spencer rolled his eyes. "Very well," he responded, without putting up a fight. "I'm not going to beg." He turned around and began pacing towards the door with Han Eden following in silence. "You pretended to go into the ashes. Well, it's time you got your wish."

This time, the Authority who had murdered Professor Prothero only minutes before, pulled out a different weapon. Kyan recognised it instantly as a flamethrower. He closed his eyes, took a breath and whispered a silent prayer.

Kyan had never been a religious man, but at this point all he could do was hope that something out there would reward him for what he had done.

As the Authority began blasting blue and red flames out from the device into Kyan's tied up body, blistering through his skin instantly, Ivan Spencer turned around and left the room. The second Authority and Han Eden swiftly followed. It was as if they couldn't even hear the young man's agonising screams.

Kyan spared one last thought for Red as his burning body began to disintegrate. He hoped more than anything that she was still alive and that she would continue their mission to bring down Ivan Spencer and his regime. To finally bring freedom to the people of The Shell.

Moments later, he was dead. Nevertheless, the Authority continued to fulfil his command of blasting the whistleblower's bones until they were reduced to nothing more than dust. Kyan was finally free from his shackles.

Walking down the narrow corridor that led out of the bloody and burning cell, Ivan Spencer spoke three simple words to his accomplices:

"Prepare for lockdown."

PART THREE

RISE OF RED

SEVENTEEN

EIGHT MONTHS LATER

Time lost all meaning in The Plant. Between the scans, check-ups and hours spent in isolation, it all became one giant haze to Red after she arrived in her cell and discovered that she was carrying a child. A child from the man she betrayed. Minutes blurred into hours, hours into days. And so on. It all became one long and mind-numbing line of moments spent in her cold, damp and uncomfortable cell.

In many ways, Red's time in The Plant made her life in The Shell feel like a distant fantasy. A safer memory, like the ones from her childhood. Somehow, both memories blurred together and felt equally as long ago. Like another lifetime, that hadn't even really existed. *Perhaps it hadn't*, Red often wondered to herself between the nightmares that kept her awake.

The only consolation, the one thing that kept Red going through the darkness and uncertainty, was the life growing inside of her.

Red had learned that this life was female. A little girl. Her daughter. Even though she'd rarely given the idea of having a child a thought, she somehow knew if she did, she would have a girl. Somehow, she'd always known.

Red had come to feel extremely attached to her unborn child. She felt her moving around inside of her during the day and she softly sang lullabies to her throughout the night. But all the while, she dreaded what the eventual outcome of her circumstance would be. She was afraid of giving birth to a child who would be taken away from her as soon as she was brought into the world. And what world was she even bringing her into? This was the thought that frightened her the most.

Red was beyond caring about her own fate. In many ways she saw her own death as the final escape. A true escape. Not like her departure from The Shell. This had simply been an escape from one hell to another. She often thought to herself how she was ready to finally leave behind the reality she had no hope left for.

But deep down, she knew that this wasn't how she truly felt. Death was the easy option. There's no way she could have allowed herself to die while her daughter remained fighting against so much evil. The evil Red had fought against herself for so long.

Despite Red's mental state, her physical health wasn't too bad. In fact, her body was in a far better condition than it had been the entire time she'd lived in The Shell. Women in The Plant were fed well and allowed plenty of time to rest to ensure the children they carried were kept in good physical shape. It was the boredom, uncertainty and isolation that made the experience as horrendous as it was.

Which is why Red became so close to her cellmate, Trip, in the time they lived together. Women in The Plant spent little time with the prisoners outside of their cells. At least any time that they were permitted to speak. So apart from the guards who patrolled the building, Trip was Red's only real companion.

Most of their conversations took place during the night. They knew that the security guards, who alternated shifts to keep watch outside the cells, often fell asleep on the job. There was no chance of the women getting out of their cells, so the guards didn't seem to worry much about nodding off.

Even so, Red and Trip figured out how to speak even quieter than whispers throughout the night. They barely spoke at all, but instead learned how to lip read. This was the time that kept them sane. The precious moments they would discuss their hopes and fears.

One of the first things Red had asked Trip during these discussions was of course about her mother. Trip hadn't known anything about her. Straight after, she'd asked her about Ethan's sister, Leyla. As she'd feared, Trip had known the girl. Or at least known of her. After several failed attempts of being artificially inseminated, she'd been met with the same fate as many other young girls who were left behind in the New Overworld.

Red had felt an overwhelming rush of sadness when Trip told her about Leyla's death. She thought back to how hopeful Ethan had been that she would still be alive. The same way Red felt about her mother. But she refused to give up believing that she would still be out there. She had to be.

But their late-night conversations weren't all negative. Red and Trip would often use this time to fantasise about someone coming to rescue them. Or even better, that they figured out a way to escape. The thought of outsmarting Carmen, the aggressive security guards and Ivan Spencer was enough to keep the two women going as the days slipped by.

This hope had nearly diminished completely. Like the last grains of sand falling through an hourglass. Until one day someone entered The Plant to turn it over, sending the sand flowing in the reverse direction. Their hope had returned, like light seeping into a once pitch-black tunnel.

She'd been an elderly lady, somewhere in her eighties. Her skin was white. Her hair the same, which was tied up in a large bun. She'd worn minimal make up, in an attempt to give off a little radiance without seeming desperate to hold on to her youth. She'd had a full figure and her clothes had been an assortment of pastels. A chunky knitted jumper and a flowing skirt. She'd worn oversized pearls.

The lady had been shown around by Carmen, who at the time was sporting two shades in her bobbed hair. One side black, the other blonde.

Whoever the lady had been and whatever the purpose of her visit, she'd exuded an air of warmth that was definitely missing in Ivan Spencer's daughter. A kindness that reached out and touched Red through the bars at the top of her cell's door.

Carmen had been walking ahead as they'd moved slowly through the corridor, staring into each cell while they drifted by. As if the women were animals in a zoo. Red couldn't even take in what Carmen was saying. She was so surprised to see someone from the outside world, particularly someone of the stranger's age. Red had realised that the lady was the first elderly person she'd seen since Marcus had passed away.

As the woman walked past Red and Trip's cell, her eyes met Red's. This brought her to a standstill. Her eyes conveyed an emotion Red couldn't work out, as if she was equally trying to read Red's thoughts. Quickly, she looked ahead at Carmen who was continuing to pace forward before diving her wrinkly hand into her bag. She pulled out a small piece of paper and practically threw it at Red through the cell's barred window. The two women disappeared around the corner and out of sight.

Red sat in silence for a few minutes, stunned. She held the piece of paper tightly in her hands, afraid the lady would change her mind and return for it. But she never came.

"Whatchya got there?" Trip had whispered.

Once completely certain the coast was clear, Red opened the wrapped up piece of paper slowly. Trip peered over her shoulder. The curiosity killing her.

The paper contained a map of the sewers in the New Overworld.

Before this day, neither Red nor Trip had given much thought to the New Overworld's infrastructure. Once they held the tiny map of its sewerage in their hands, it seemed painstakingly obvious what they had to do. They needed to somehow escape their cell and climb up through the sewers to the New Overworld.

As the days and weeks began to pass after the mystery guest had swiftly floated through The Plant, offering what appeared to be an escape from their current nightmare, Red and Trip waited until late at night to discuss their exit strategy. They sketched out diagrams of how they thought it would be possible to escape through the pipes in The Plant.

It appeared that the route on the map led up into a house, which both women decided must be the old lady's home. Or at least some sort of place of refuge. Either that or it was just a trap. A hell that led to yet another hell, a pattern Red had grown accustomed to by now. But both Red and Trip decided that the risk was worth taking. It was worth it for the sake of their children.

The determined pair's plan was to escape The Shell as soon as they had both given birth. Not only because they were due around the same time, but because of how closely attached they had grown to one another. They had become like sisters. A feeling Red could only ever compare to her relationship with Delta.

It was this exact plan that Red and Trip had been discussing the day Red's water broke. Three weeks early.

EIGHTEEN

In the eight months that had passed since Red had arrived at The Plant, so much had changed down in the world she'd left behind. Since Kyan leaked the truth about the Overworld on Shareflow, an uprising began to occur in The Shell. Or at least, it had tried to.

It hadn't taken long before word of the *hoax apocalypse* had rippled throughout the United Underworld. So much so that it led to Ivan Spencer and his regime tightening up security more than ever before. Authorities, who'd rarely been seen patrolling the streets prior to the leak, were everywhere at this point. Clusters of the uniformed men were seen on every tattered street corner of The Shell.

These Authorities had also become more aggressive and sometimes violent. There had been several incidents of citizens coming together and peacefully protesting, before the Authorities had attacked them with riot gear and pepper spray.

One man had even been killed in a brawl that had got out of hand with a pair of Authorities. But as usual, there had been no trials following the innocent man's death.

It was rumoured that the exit zone had been sealed off completely in reaction to Kyan being able to escape The Shell so easily. Although some people were sure it couldn't be, as cargo was still transported to and from the Overworld. But whether this was true or not was irrelevant, considering the sheer amount of Authorities that were guarding the Docklands.

Despite all of Ivan Spencer's attempts to conceal the truth, citizens were growing more and more angry and frustrated. They were demanding answers that weren't being given to them. Their leader knew that increasing security alone wasn't going to stop this. The damage had already been done.

The determined dictator continued to explain in televised transmissions across The Shell how everyone would eventually join him, his family and the government in the New Overworld. The government began to release genuine footage of the New Overworld for the first time ever, but this simply made citizens more upset and enraged at the world they were missing out on.

Propaganda was played across all networks in The Shell on repeat, with Ivan Spencer's monotone voice constantly pulsating throughout its bleak and desolate streets. He made promises as to how change was coming, before hypnotic music concluded each broadcast.

In other frequent televised propaganda, an actor was used to play Kyan who had been arrested and was being kept in an empty white room to be questioned. In this footage the fake Kyan spoke through tears as to how he'd made the leak up and was a traitor to the people of The Shell.

Ivan Spencer denied Kyan's statement since the day of the leak, labelling his ex-colleague a rebel and a terrorist. He explained how Kyan's words had been empty allegations, fabricated to stir up trouble and encourage rebellion. Which was exactly what they had started to do.

Everywhere you looked in The Shell there were posters of the man who played Kyan in the video footage. His name spray-painted across walls down every backstreet. On buildings, pods and all along the banks of the River Tamesis. Even when Authorities tore down the posters and painted over the graffiti, they would both re-emerge in the dead of night. People were willing to risk their lives just to express their support for Kyan and his bravery.

Ivan Spencer's attempts to turn people against the young activist had backfired on him and turned the fake Kyan into a martyr. A symbol of hope for change and for escape. For revolution. Citizens saw right through the fact the man on the screen felt remorseful for what he had done. They knew that he had either been drugged or held at gunpoint. It would take a lot more for the people of the United Underworld to change their minds.

But despite this, the majority of the people in The Shell continued to carry out their day jobs working at the Reactor. What choice did they have? The presence of Authorities had been heightened and curfews had been created in many areas in an attempt to prevent citizens from being out at night.

People still needed to earn money, as minimal as it was, making it even harder to revolt. But there was a real feeling in the air that change was coming. And it was clear that Ivan Spencer could feel it too.

Although the man employed to play the activist in the propaganda clips very closely resembled Kyan, anyone who had actually known him would have been able to tell right away it wasn't him. While Kyan didn't have many friends – he spent his entire life outside of the United Underworld Studios dedicated to Shareflow – one of the few people who knew what he really looked like was Ethan.

Ethan had seen Kyan's face clearer than daylight on the day he'd taken off his Authority mask in front of him. This made him certain that Kyan was dead, meaning he'd died trying to fight for answers. He had sacrificed his life trying to find the woman Ethan loved. This made Ethan more determined than ever to continue the legacy both Red and Kyan had left behind. But there was no way he'd given in to the idea that Red was dead.

Using this knowledge that the man posing as Kyan in the propaganda videos was actually a fraud, Ethan had formed an underground alliance with Delta and Xavier, seeking to recruit other rebels to form a secret army. The trio's plan was to build the army large enough to fight back against Ivan Spencer's regime.

Although this was how Ethan was spending his spare time, he was still having to put up an act that he was working as a therapist and treating Red. He had no choice. He needed to ensure his commander, Eric Vineyard, wouldn't suspect his patient was missing. Under no circumstances could he find this out. That would be the end of both Ethan and Red.

At the same time that his missing patient was going into labour in the world above, preparing to give birth to his child, a group of Authorities approached the hideout of Ethan, Delta and Xavier's secret alliance. Dressed in their full white uniforms, the masked men clutched their weapons as they approached the entrance of the bunker.

"Uh oh. Authorities!" Delta spat as she peered through one of the hideout's grimy blacked-out windows.

"What? Where?" Ethan replied, springing up from where he was sitting.

"Out-side," Delta said, fear visible in her voice as she broke the word in two.

"Grab your weapons!" Ethan called out before a group of rebels, including Xavier, ran in from another room.

There was a loud bang on the door.

Ethan picked up a large laser sniper and signalled the others to do the same.

"Come on, guys. We can't be afraid."

"Wait!" said Delta abruptly. "They're placing their weapons on the ground... with their hands in the air!"

Ethan scrambled next to Delta to see if what she was saying was really true. To the young therapist's surprise, the Authorities had placed their weapons on the ground and were holding their hands above their heads. A pang of paranoia ran through Ethan's veins.

"It must be a trap," he said swiftly. "Proceed with caution!"

As if they'd read his mind, one by one the Authorities

began removing their masks. There were eight men in total standing outside the bunker with their faces exposed. Authorities never revealed their identities.

"We come in peace!" the man standing at the front called out. He looked like the leader of the group. The man had dull skin, ashy-blonde hair and faded blue eyes. He didn't look threatening. There was something about his eyes that assured Ethan. A purity.

After waiting for at least another thirty seconds, Ethan made his decision.

"Let them in."

NINETEEN

All of Red's surroundings melted into a blurry haze as she was wheeled into the room she was to give birth in. Like ice turning into water. The sounds that surrounded her faded out into a distant static noise. Voices into far off slurs.

Despite the fact that Red had experienced so much suffering in her life, giving birth was a completely new type of pain. Not simply because of what she was experiencing physically, but through the emotions that were stirring within her at the thought of bringing a child into such a dark, dismal and uncertain existence. Into a world where her father doesn't even know she exists.

These thoughts plagued Red's mind as she lay on her back, legs spread widely apart. Pushing with all her might. There was no hand for her to hold as the sweat dripped down the sides of her shaved head. Clothed in clinical white, Red shut her eyes and screamed.

Each hour that passed blended into the next like waves crashing into one another. Until finally, somewhere within the twelfth hour, she heard three words through the static.

"There's the head."

What happened next was even more of a blur. Once Red's baby's head was out, the rest of her body followed very quickly. And once she was out, the child was given a tag on her right leg that read *57821*. This would be her name.

Children were given numbers instead of names in The Plant, as if to avoid any notion of personalisation. As if they were cattle. Red hadn't even considered what she would call her little girl. She hadn't wanted to allow herself to become too attached, but it was too late for that by now.

She'd spoken to her daughter during the night. She'd felt her moving around inside her. Kicking her. Growing within her. All of this happened up to the moment she finally gave birth to her.

All she wanted to do was to hold her child. To see her at the very least. But neither of these wishes were granted. Red's daughter was taken away from her the moment she was born into the world.

"No!" Red screamed out at the top of her lungs. A paramedic wrapped his bony fingers around her mouth to prevent her from screaming again.

The agony Red felt as her daughter was stolen from her, right in front of her eyes, outweighed all of the pain she'd experienced giving birth. It was as if her heart had been pulled straight out of her chest and thrown onto the floor in front of her.

She didn't even feel the sharp jab of the injection in her thigh through her tears. Within moments she passed out.

* * *

As Ethan approached the government district where he was to meet with Eric Vineyard, all he could think about was the Authorities who had turned up at the front door of his underground alliance's bunker.

The Authorities had decided to rebel against the government and join Ethan's alliance. This wasn't the first time this had happened. Many Authorities were beginning to mistrust Ivan Spencer and his regime and were worried about their own futures. But this was definitely the largest group of Authorities that had decided to join the rebels.

As always, Ethan made sure to arrive at least ten minutes before Eric. His boss did not like to be kept waiting, even for a couple of minutes, so Ethan decided it was better just to make sure he was already there when his commander arrived.

The location the pair met every week was the same restaurant Eric had lost his temper eight months prior, demanding that Ethan kept him regularly updated with Red's progress. Ethan had carried out this order, despite the fact that everything he fed back to his boss was a lie.

Not only was Ethan keeping from Eric that his patient had escaped The Shell, he was also hiding that he was heading up one of the most wanted underground rebel alliances in the United Underworld. And, if those Authorities had managed to find where they were so easily, surely the government wouldn't be far behind.

Every time Ethan met with Eric, his stomach churned at the thought of being discovered and told he would be executed. But it turned out the news on this particular day would be far from the bleak fate he was constantly expecting.

Much to Ethan's surprise, "I want to thank you" were the words Eric Vineyard spoke to begin their meeting over lunch. He then went on to say:

"It's been a tumultuous time over the past eight months, since those twisted lies were leaked across the United Underworld. But you have stood strong, defiant. Closed your ears and eyes to the noise and continued to focus on the task at hand. So thank you."

Ethan couldn't believe what he was hearing. He had never heard his commander speak with any sort of human emotion, let alone the expression of gratitude. It seemed too good to be true, so he decided it probably was. Perhaps this was a test? A mind game he was playing. For the moment, Ethan just decided to keep quiet and listen.

"Now, as a reward for this commitment and dedication," Eric continued, "I want to take you to the New Overworld. To show you how far it has come along."

Ethan's shock transformed into a wave of excitement and euphoria. Could this really be happening? This could finally be his chance to find and rescue Red!

"R-really?" he stuttered in response. "You really want me to come up there?" Ethan was aware he was letting his guard down but he was feeling far too vulnerable to contain himself.

"Yes, the time is right," Eric replied, the scar tightening on his face as he attempted a smile. It was more of a grimace, forced and uncomfortable.

Ethan quickly pulled himself together. He straightened his back, cleared his throat and spoke clearly:

"That's great news, sir. My commitment to the government will continue for as long as I'm on this earth. It is a pleasure and privilege to be of your service. So, when do you want to leave?"

"Pack tonight," Eric replied, suddenly steely. "We'll leave first thing in the morning."

It then dawned on Ethan what he was about to sacrifice. How he was about to put both his and the life of Red, if she even was still alive, at risk. He then took a moment to consider the bravery and strength she'd shown escaping The Shell in the first place. It was his turn to rise up. There was no going back.

* * *

Red's eyes fluttered a few times. Her lashes like moths in the darkness. She finally opened them wide and realised that she was back in her cell. Trip was sitting behind her, her face filled with sympathy. Like a mother's expression when her child has fallen over and cut their knees.

Red winced as she felt a dull pain throb and pulsate through her body. She hadn't been given enough time to rest and recover before she was ruthlessly thrown out of the ward. Carmen and her officials obviously needed the bed for the next victim.

But there was another kind of pain Red was feeling. Worse than physical. An emptiness she'd never experienced before. It was different to how she'd longed to be reunited with Ethan since escaping The Shell. It was even different to the pain and longing she felt when she lost both her parents at such a young age.

The loss she was feeling for her newborn daughter, who she didn't even get the chance to hold, outweighed all the other pain she'd ever felt. Like an organ had been removed from her body that she didn't even know existed. An organ she was unable to live without.

"I'm so sorry, Red," said Trip, smoothing her hand across her friend's shaved head. "I can only imagine what you're goin' through right now."

Red was going to answer back, say something cutting like "you'd never understand," but stopped herself when she realised that Trip would be experiencing the very same emotions soon. Instead she decided to say nothing.

After a silence that seemed to last forever, Trip spoke again. This time slowly and carefully choosing her words:

"I did some thinkin' while you were away, Red. And I know this is th' last thing you'll want to be hearin' right now. But th' truth is, now you've given birth they'll be inseminatin' you again after thirty days. I might not've even given birth in that time!"

Red knew what was coming.

"I think you should go ahead without me, Red," Trip said firmly. "I think you should carry out our plans as soon as you can, on your own."

Red shook her head, before replying: "Not without you. We're doing this together."

They had made a promise to each other that they would only attempt an escape from The Plant if they were able to leave as a pair.

"I know we promised, Red," Trip replied compassionately. "But the time for you is now. I would only slow you down. I can stay 'ere and keep those bastards distracted."

She knew there was some sense in what her cellmate was saying, but when it came to being stubborn, Red was hard to beat.

"If I have thirty days then that's thirty more days in which you might give birth. Then we can go together." Red's tone implied that she wasn't going to be convinced otherwise.

Trip took a deep breath, before placing her hand over her heavily-pregnant stomach. She then spoke three simple words:

"Let's leave tonight."

Red's eyes widened in surprise. Had she really just heard her friend correctly? It took her a few moments before she was able to respond.

"Trip, you can't come with me. You're in no physical state—"

Trip cut Red off before she could finish her sentence. "I'm willin' to take the risk. What 'ave I got to lose? I can die tryin' to escape or die down 'ere after givin' birth more times than my body can take." This time it was Trip who sounded like her mind was made up and her decision was not up for debate.

"Besides," she continued, "I can see in your eyes just 'ow cut up you are over your child. That's probably th' main reason you wanted to stay 'ere longer, knowin' that you're closer to 'er."

Red opened her mouth to retaliate but Trip continued her explanation:

"I know this is gonna sound ruthless, Red. But our situations are different. Your child is the daughter of someone you care about. I know this because I've 'eard the way you've spoken 'bout Ethan these past eight months. I know you don't like to admit it. And I get that. You don't like openin' up about your emotions. I'm the same. But I know you more than you realise. That little girl was made from love, which is the reason we're gonna escape from 'ere, then come back and get 'er."

Red shook her head, tears welling up in her eyes. She didn't want to accept and admit to herself that what Trip was saying was the truth. But deep down, she knew it was. Instead she just said:

"But what about your child, Trip? The map that shows how to escape the sewers shows what an intricate and complicated system it is up there. You'd be putting your son's life at an extreme risk–" once again Trip cut her friend off.

"This is what I was gettin' to if you'd let me finish," she said abruptly. "Your child was created from love, whereas mine's been created from evil. You think I care about this life growing inside me? You think I want to bring it into this world?"

Red wiped her own tears and put her arm around Trip to comfort her.

"You say that now, but you have no idea how you'll feel about him once he's born. It doesn't matter where he's come from. The fact is he's here now." Red looked into her cellmate's eyes to put emphasis on what she'd just said.

Trip continued to stare forward blankly.

"It's a risk I'm willin' to take," she said. "Let's get everything prepared: we're leaving as soon as the last guards have carried out their checks."

After that, there was nothing left to be said. The decision had already been made.

* * *

Ethan arrived back to the hideout of the rebellion just as the artificial night was about to fall, hardly able to contain his excitement. He still couldn't believe his luck. Although, he was equally as terrified. What would he actually do once he got up to the New Overworld?

Would he attempt to murder Eric before he made his escape? And even if he got that far, how would he get past the rest of his commander's security? What if he somehow managed to get past them too, where would he even go? He had no idea where Red could be, if she was even still alive. He had to keep believing she was.

Ethan was greeted by Delta, Xavier and the rest of his army of rebels, including the newest recruits: the ex-Authorities. The therapist gathered everyone into one room to pass on his big news:

"It fills me with such excitement to inform you of today's developments. Due to the fact I've been living up to the expectations of my commander, Eric Vineyard, he is rewarding me by giving me a tour of the New Overworld tomorrow. I have agreed and am going to take this opportunity to find Red. In the meantime, I want you all to stay here, lay low and keep building on our army."

The room erupted into applause.

Ethan broke out into a smile. Which then led to a loud and infectious laugh. For the first time in a long time, he felt happy. And for the first time in his life, he felt like a leader.

TWENTY

Red and Trip knew their chance to escape was fast approaching as night fell on The Plant. The guards had carried out their final checks for the night. *It's now or never*, Red thought.

In the months after Red had been given the mysterious map, a lot of groundwork had taken place. Much of this preparation had been inspired by a historical story Red had once read in a book Marcus had given to her from the twentieth century. The book had told the story of three American criminals who had managed to escape from a prison on an island called Alcatraz.

Red remembered reading with amazement how the men had fabricated dummy heads from a mixture of soap, toilet paper and their own hair, before leaving them in their beds to trick the prison officers who would make their nightly inspections.

The two women mirrored this technique entirely. The only

part they didn't need to worry about was saving masses of cut hair, seeing as their hair was kept sheared anyway. A sprinkle of shavings across their dummy heads did the trick.

And just like the prisoners of Alcatraz before them, Red and Trip had used utensils such as spoons to help them chisel away the moisture-damaged concrete from around the air vent in their room. They had waited until early evening each night, just before dinner was brought to them, to carry out their chiselling.

This was when a loud and monotonous speech from Ivan Spencer was played through small speakers in every cell. His droning voice hypnotic, as always. Red and Trip seized this opportunity every evening, as they knew guards very rarely patrolled the corridors during this time. But they always made sure to take it in turns to chip while the other kept watch. Just in case.

There were a few occasions when both Red and Trip were sure that other cellmates had heard them. Despite their cell being positioned where they couldn't *see* their fellow prisoners, they were close enough to be able to hear them through the walls. But even in those moments, when both of them and their nearby cellmates would fall quiet for what felt like minutes, there was a feeling in the air that both Red and Trip didn't need to panic.

Because the truth was, although the women throughout The Plant didn't get the chance to speak to one another, there was an unspoken connection between all of them. A sisterhood. A bond that only they would be able to share. Even if any of them were to make it out alive, the bond would never be broken.

Even if one of the women knew that a fellow prisoner was attempting to escape, they would do nothing. They wouldn't do anything because they were secretly wishing that someone else had the guts to do it. They were hoping that their cellmates would successfully escape so they could go get help. Then the whole nightmare would be over.

This gave the women of The Plant hope.

When the night finally arrived that Red and Trip knew was their opportunity to escape, they didn't waste a moment worrying about being heard by their inmates. In many ways they hoped they would hear them. That way they would know help was coming and they would have the hope they so needed.

As the final inspections of the night drew to a close, Red and Trip barely waited another few minutes before they took a deep breath and removed the vent that covered the hole they had dug into the wall that lead to the sewers of The Plant.

Carrying nothing but a small rucksack which contained a flask filled with water, some scraps of food they had managed to keep hidden away and the map they hoped would lead to their salvation, Red led the way as she crawled through the hole in the wall, onwards into the dark damp skeleton of their prison.

Once through, Red slowly helped Trip do the same. Being heavily pregnant, Trip knew she was going to have to rely on Red's help a lot through their quest. But she was determined to avoid this as much as possible.

The two women quietly shut the vent back onto the wall

behind them, before they began to climb through a large red pipe, which according to their map, ran down vertically for at least a mile. This would be the easy part.

"I can't believe this is actually 'appenin'," said Trip.

Red looked up at her brave friend and broke into a smile.

"It's funny," she whispered. "I kinda can. I seem to be making a habit of escaping from bad situations these days."

Trip smiled back as she stared down at the rebellious soul. Her smile quickly vanished as she looked beyond her friend at the vast drop into the darkness beneath them.

"C'mon," she said. "We're not out yet."

Time seemed to slow right down as Red and Trip carried out their mission to escape The Plant. This wasn't entirely a bad thing for the pair. As soon as morning came and the guards discovered dummies inside their cell beds, they knew that the government would be coming for them. They needed to reach their destination as soon as possible.

The trouble was, the women had to climb as slowly as they could. Not only because one of them was eight months pregnant. But because if they went too fast, they would slip and fall. And it was already a long way down.

Eventually, the duo reached an area where the thick red pipe curved and continued horizontally. This was where Red and Trip knew they had to change course slightly. The map displayed how they would have to crawl out of the red pipe through a small hatch. They would then have to crawl across a set of thin pipes with wide gaps in between and a drop beneath. Eventually they would reach a final vertical pipe that would lead them on to their destination. Whatever that might be.

Coated in sweat, their breathing rapid with fear, the two determined women slowly crawled along the thin pipes. In complete silence, Red realised that her surroundings were spinning.

Oh shit, she thought to herself. *Vertigo.*

Red had always been scared of heights. As a child she would even grow dizzy when her father carried her on his shoulders. When she first started riding in pods as a teenager in The Shell, she always navigated away from the high tracks to avoid the nauseous feeling.

But in recent times, Red had seemed to overcome her fear. Perhaps considering everything else she'd been through – from murdering another human being and escaping the hell of The Shell, to giving birth to her first child who was immediately taken away from her – heights were the least of her worries.

But as Red crawled across the thin metal pipe in the dark, trying to be as quiet as possible, she couldn't help but worry that she would slip and fall to her doom. Worried that she would knock into her pregnant friend and take her plummeting down with her.

"Red, are you all right?" Trip asked, as if she read her mind. When Red didn't reply, it was Trip who quickly became afraid. "Red!?"

Red's dizziness snapped back into focus, knocking her off balance and causing her hands to slip. It was as if time moved in slow motion as she fell backwards and screamed into the darkness.

Trip reacted instantly. She launched out and grabbed her friend by the ankle. She wrapped her own legs around the pipe as tightly as possible to prevent them both from falling.

Red dangled head first, her blood rushing to her head. She opened her mouth to scream again but only managed a croak that turned into a whisper.

"I've got you!" Trip yelled down to her friend.

But already she could feel Red slipping from her grasp. She wouldn't be able to hold on for much longer. The rucksack Red had been carrying fell from her back, along with their flask of water, scraps of food — and most importantly: the map.

As Red hung face down, staring into the pitch-black abyss beneath her, she felt her life flash before her. All of the darkness. The lack of sunlight on her face, which she'd craved for years. Why had it been this way? From one prison to the next. Why had the people she loved been taken from her one by one? Her father. Her mother. What had she done to deserve this torture?

But just as she felt herself slipping away into her own tunnel of sorrow and self-pity, a rush of adrenaline swept through Red's veins as she began to look outside of herself. She thought of all the other innocent people back in The Shell, being forced to live hidden away from the world. Forced to live a life in darkness.

She thought of Delta. Of Ethan.

She then thought of all the women in The Plant that were forced to carry children inside them before giving the innocent newborns away to the evil hands of the government, including her own. How could she give up and allow her daughter to live through the same misery she had in the hands of Ivan Spencer and his regime?

She wouldn't let it. The cycle would end here.

Red used all her adrenaline and strength to rise up. She had no choice but to use her still-swollen abdominal muscles to reach and grab the hand Trip wasn't using to hold onto her ankle. She had to do this slowly as not to pull Trip off. In agony, Red reached up and grabbed onto Trip's arm. Both women gave out a small yell of relief as their hands met and clutched tightly. Trip let go of Red's ankle and used both of her hands to hold onto Reds'.

It was Trip's turn to be strong. Eight months pregnant and already exhausted from the climb, she knew she would have to use all the physical capabilities she had to not only save both of their lives, but the lives of all the prisoners in The Plant and The Shell.

And Trip was not one to give up without a fight.

Trip used all of her might to pull herself up lifting Red with her. She kept her legs wrapped around the pipe as tightly as she could. As she did this, she felt an agonising pain inside her stomach that she knew was bad news. But there was nothing she could do. Her choices were to let go and allow both of them to fall, or to keep hoisting upwards.

As the world went into slow motion once more, Trip knew in her heart what she was doing. She knew that by attempting to save both Red and herself, she was sacrificing the life that was growing inside of her. The truth was, she'd known she was taking that risk the moment she crawled out of her cell. And as she'd already decided, it was a sacrifice she was willing to make. A sacrifice to save humanity.

Ignoring what felt like a knife slicing through the inside of her stomach, Trip used every ounce of adrenaline she could muster to pull both Red and herself up towards safety. This time it worked.

Trip lifted Red with her until both women were able to wrap their entire bodies around the thin horizontal pipe above them. Once safe to let go of each other's hands, Red and Trip hugged onto the pipe like children holding onto their mothers. Their bodies shook with fear and were coated with sweat.

Red could feel her heart beating loudly in her chest against the metallic pole. Tears were streaming down her face even though she wasn't crying. Tears of fear. Tears of shock. Tears of happiness that she was alive.

Slowly, Red looked up to Trip who was in front of her by this point. She opened her mouth to say thank you, but saw Trip was already moving forwards.

"Come on, Red," she said. "We need t'continue."

Red said nothing, instead she simply nodded her head in approval. She began to slowly crawl forward once more. This time the dizziness was gone. This time she wouldn't lose her balance.

* * *

Eventually, the pair reached the end of the set of thin pipes, which brought them to a row of twelve thick cylinders running vertically, just as the map had shown. There was a thin ledge beneath the pipes, which the women stood on. If Red's memory of what the map had said served her correctly, they had to take the seventh tube from the left.

In the near-pitch-black surrounding, Red tried to count the

pipes. She couldn't see the first one through the darkness. It was too risky to walk along the ledge to check, so she blinked repeatedly, trying to make her eyes adjust to the darkness. She focused on what she thought was the first pipe and started counting. *One, two, three…* She got up to the tube they were currently standing beneath. It was the fifth one in.

"C'mon, it's that pipe we need to climb up," Red said. As she pointed, Red noticed her hands were not only wet from sweat, but covered with something dark and sticky. She recognised the metallic smell and turned to Trip.

"Trip!" Red called out with terror. "You're bleeding!"

Trip sat herself upright, her back to one of the thick vertical pipes, which had fragments of rust running all the way across it.

"Where?" Red continued, although she was sure she already knew. She pulled herself upwards and faced her friend directly.

"You know where," Trip replied.

"Why didn't you tell me?" Red asked, unable to hide her dismay.

"And then what? What could you 'ave done?" she responded, her voice revealing the physical pain she was in. "There would 'ave bin nothin' you could've done, so I didn't wanna worry you. I knew we 'ad to keep goin'. We just 'ad to keep movin'."

Red felt a rush of guilt pulsate through her body as she realised what her vertigo may have cost her friend. She didn't even need to say the words. Trip could see it on her face.

"Don't, Red," she said plainly, before continuing:

"I told you before we set off that I knew what I was riskin'. We've come this far. We need to finish our mission. Course it could all end badly. P'rhaps we're being led into a trap. But what could we 'ave done? Stayed down there forever? Waited until we weren't able to pump out any more children before facing execution? C'mon, Red. You're stronger than that. This isn't just about us anymore. This is about them, down there. And up there."

No sooner had she mouthed the words before Red picked herself up, wiped away her tears and covered her emotions with a stern look. An expression Trip hadn't seen on her friend before. Her piercing green eyes stared forward blankly, as if she'd pulled shutters down over her soul's windows.

It was the expression she had when her mother was left above in the Old World. One she'd turned to when her bookstore had burnt down and when Marcus had died in front of her. It was also the expression she had when she drugged the man she'd fallen for. And when she'd shot down the Authority who had tried to prevent her from escaping.

This was Red's battle expression. One that signified she was ready for whatever faced her. Ready for war. It was the armour she'd built as a child and turned to whenever she felt numb. Whenever she was unable to process the emotions building up inside her.

"Come on then," she said with an icy tone. "Let's finish this once and for all."

They crawled along the ledge to what Red thought was the seventh pipe. *God, I hope I'm right*, she thought, praying that the map had said seventh and that she'd counted correctly. Only time would tell.

With that, the two began to climb the rungs that would lead them up the thick pipe and on to the final part of their mission. They did this without speaking another word for the next hour or so until they reached the vent.

Red clenched her fist and drew it back, then sent it flying through the small square in the darkness. The vent's metal covering fell away effortlessly, as if it wasn't even secured in place.

A sudden bright light filtered through the gap in the wall. Red's eyes flickered as they adjusted to regain vision. Through the brightness, she could make out what looked like an old-fashioned room. A room that belonged to the Old World. In a similar style to the room she lived in as a child.

And then, a voice. The women heard an old man's voice.

"Vera... they're here! Red's here!"

TWENTY-ONE

Nothing could have prepared Red for all the things she would soon discover. So many answers that she'd been waiting for her entire life were finally in reach, but at this stage she still didn't know it.

Climbing through the small vent with help from the elderly man, both Red and Trip landed one by one onto the soft carpet. After so many years of hard concrete floors, it felt like falling into a cloud for the two women.

Vera walked into the room and Red instantly recognised her as the old lady that had visited The Plant. Once again, she was dressed in chalky pastel-hued knits. Her thin white hair tied back into a tight bun.

"We've been expecting you," she said.

The two young women couldn't believe their ears. After spending so much time worrying that their journey would all be in vain, those four words proved instantly that Vera had every intention of leading Red to her home.

But before the elderly couple could even contemplate explaining anything to the two women, helping Trip was the number one priority. Henry quickly carried her into a bedroom while Vera ran to grab towels and water. Trip began panting in pain. She had to start pushing.

Red crouched down and squeezed her friend's hand tightly. Everyone in the room knew what was coming, but didn't want to say it out loud. It was time for a young woman to simply be by her friend's side during her time of need. And she would stay there every step of the way.

Surrounded by bloodied towels, Trip had given birth to her dead child.

Vera held the stillborn in her arms. "My dear, I am so so sorry," she said softly. "Would you like to hold him and say goodbye?"

Trip shut her eyes, turned her head to the side and shook her head. Vera paused for a moment, but then walked out of the room.

"I understand."

Red wrapped her arms around her friend and cried. But no tears came from Trip.

"No, Red," she said. "Please don't do this. I'm ok. I'll honestly be fine. I jus' need t'rest."

Red sat upright and wiped her eyes. She nodded.

"Just call me if you need me."

Red and Henry left the room in silence. Trip was relieved to finally be alone.

* * *

"I think it's time you learned some answers," Vera said directly to Red, in her softly-spoken voice. "I'm sure you're more than ready to hear them."

To their surprise, Trip entered the room and sat down beside Red. She clutched her hand tightly for reassurance. It was like she was already arming herself for what she was about to hear. Her intuition told her it wouldn't be positive.

It was only an hour after Trip had given birth to her dead son, enough time to have washed herself, but not to have slept. Red had also showered, but couldn't even contemplate sleeping without hearing what the elderly couple had to say.

Vera took a sip of the tea from her bone-white ivory cup. She then drew back a deep breath before beginning her story:

"Now first of all, we need to make one thing clear. Although Henry and I are related to Ivan Spencer by blood, we completely disagree with what he is doing. He took the development plans his father had started and twisted them to carry out his own evil vision. We promise to help you both as much as we can. But we need you to understand the truth about what has happened and what is happening now.

"First things first, you've probably worked this out already on your own, but the asteroid that was supposed to have hit the earth over a decade ago, never really existed. It was an elaborate series of real-life special effects – including a hologram that was projected across the sky – to convince humanity that we needed to be transported down to The Shell.

"Due to the planet's overcrowded population, Ivan's plan

was to wipe people out over time once they were in the United Underworld. But before he did this, he decided to use them to send power up to the New Overworld. This is where he plans to develop a new population. Aside from his family and the government, the children being produced at The Plant are the only current residents of the New Overworld."

Vera stopped speaking for a moment before her wrinkled face glazed over with guilt. And then, her eyes became glassy through her tears. Before Red had a chance to speak she continued:

"I know what you're thinking. Why didn't we do anything? Why didn't we speak up? We wanted to. We're his own flesh and blood and we hate him for what he's done. For what he's doing. For what his father started…"

Vera couldn't continue any longer as her words became a whisper and she broke down into tears. Henry quickly put his arm around his wife and continued for her.

"We didn't do anything because we were afraid, Red. All of us were. All of us still are. That's why we need you. That's why we need you to not be afraid. Just like your mother wouldn't have been."

A chill was sent spiralling through Red's veins like electricity through a network of cables. How did this old man know anything about her mother? And, more importantly, why was he speaking about her in past tense?

As if hearing Red's thoughts, Vera wiped away her tears and resumed her story:

"Ivan met your mother through your father, Red. As you know, your dad worked for the government for many years before he died. In this time, Ivan had spent a lot of time with your mother and fallen for her very heavily. So much so, that he had your father killed to allow him to pursue a relationship with her."

Red's heart stopped. She'd played out so many scenarios throughout her life about what the truth could have been. But nothing prepared her for this. As much as each word felt like a piece of burning coal being pushed against her bare flesh, Red needed to hear more. She just had to keep on listening. Like an addict waiting for her next fix, she demanded Vera to continue.

"Keep going. I need to know everything," she hissed through gritted teeth.

Trip reached forward and grabbed her friend's other hand. "You don't need to hear more right now," Trip said. "We should rest, it's bin a long, long day—"

"I need to hear everything!" Red retaliated in a venomous tone.

Vera took another deep breath, before continuing slowly.

"It's ok, Trip. I understand she needs to know more. I would want the same."

Trip released her grip from Red's left hand, but continued to hold onto her right tightly. She then nodded in agreement, knowing that she would also feel exactly the same. Besides, she wanted to know more herself.

"As much as I hate to share the next part of this story with you, I know that it's something that needs to be done. You've suffered enough already, dear." Vera's tone was warm and velvety, before it turned as cold as snow as she continued the tale:

"Your mother did in fact begin a secret relationship with Ivan. So secret at this stage that nobody knew about it, not even us. One thing I do know though, looking back now, is that your mother never loved him. It was a relationship built upon fear. Fear for your safety more than anything. Which is why she knew she had to go along with his wishes."

This time, it was Red who felt the guilt rush through her like water running down a stream. Was all of this her fault? If it weren't for her existence, her mother wouldn't have had to go along with Ivan Spencer's vile demands. Red hated him more in this moment than she ever had before.

Vera continued, warning Red once again to brace herself for what she was about to hear:

"When Ivan plotted the asteroid hoax, he had told your mother how she was to join him in the New Overworld. Now Red, this is hard for me to explain but Ivan had resented you, as you weren't his own daughter. We never knew who he had Carmen with, nobody did, but the fact that the girl is his own flesh and blood is obviously why he is so devoted to her. In many ways, it seemed like he had wanted your mother to be a mother to her."

Red felt sick to the stomach at the thought of her mother being forced to act as a guardian to Carmen. She also felt a pang of jealousy towards Ivan Spencer's daughter as she realised how she would have spent time with her mother when it should have been her. Vera continued, this time softly placing her bony hand on the confused young woman's shoulder as she spoke:

"Now what you have to understand here, Red, is that your

mother made each decision with your best interests in mind. When it came to making the choice to leave you behind in The Shell, this was simply out of a compromise to keep you alive.

From what we heard through whispers within the family, Ivan had planned to have you killed. Your mother compromised with him, saying she would stay with him in the New Overworld by choice, acting as a mother to Carmen, providing he granted her one wish. To allow you to stay down in The Shell.

Now, we know that your mother knew of Ivan's eventual intentions when it came to the people of the United Underworld, which is why we never doubted for a second that her ambition was to escape Ivan's control and come to your rescue."

Red could hold it in no longer. Her emotions came to the surface like boiling water frothing out from a pan.

"She's dead, isn't she!?" Red screamed, each word filled with pain. "Just tell me now, is my mother dead?"

Vera closed her eyes, but tears still managed to escape them and splatter down across her cheeks. She took a quick short breath, before nodding her head and opening her eyes:

"Yes, dear. Your mother is dead."

All that was left of Red's world shattered around her into tiny fragments. Like a bolt of lightning penetrating a house made entirely of glass.

TWENTY-TWO

Ethan opened his eyes and checked his connecter instantly. As hoped, he had woken to a message from Eric Vineyard telling him they would be heading to the New Overworld that morning.

The young man jumped out of bed, had a speedy shower and got dressed into his uniform. He then began to pack his bag, trying to slow down the anxious thoughts running through his mind. This was his one chance to get up to the New Overworld and hopefully find out whether Red was still alive.

He wasn't prepared to even entertain the thought that she wasn't.

At the same moment Ethan rushed around his flat, waiting to be picked up by his commander, the guards in The Plant were discovering the two dummies inside Red and Trip's cell.

"What!?" Carmen shrieked as she was informed of the news. "How did you manage to let this happen?"

The two guards stood in silence, completely dumbfounded themselves that the two women had managed to escape right in front of their noses.

"I don't want my father to find out about this yet," Carmen continued. "It's not worth making him upset. I want you to send up a small group of officials to discreetly find those two girls and bring them back to me. Alive."

The two guards nodded but still stood in silence.

"Well, what are you waiting for? Go!" Carmen spat with rage. With that, the two men twisted round on their heels and darted towards the door.

"Besides," Carmen continued quietly as she stood on her own. "They won't get very far out there."

* * *

Vera brought another mug of tea into the room and placed it on the table in front of Red. Although just like the last one, it remained untouched so had to be tipped away after it grew cold.

Red had sat in silence for nearly three hours. Trip, while still exhausted and in pain from her stillbirth, managed to eat a few slices of toast for breakfast and down two mugs of coffee. It had been so long since she'd been able to eat anything that wasn't gruel and drink anything that wasn't stale water, so she savoured every mouthful.

Red, on the other hand, had no appetite at all. The way she felt now, she wondered if she would ever eat again.

The three women had been up all night. Henry went to bed about forty-five minutes after Vera had delivered the devastating news to Red. The young woman had sat in silence, simply staring blankly at the wall. Henry knew nothing he could say would help with what she was feeling, so he went to sleep after fatigue started to kick in.

Realising that her sympathetic words were being spoken in vain, Vera would be next to head to bed.

"I must try and get a few hours of shut-eye," she said to the two women. "I have a feeling today is going to be a long day and I need my strength. Help yourselves to anything but please, whatever you do, stay down here."

Before the old woman had the chance to leave, Trip had a question she desperately needed answering. "Wait, Vera," she said. "How did you know Red was at The Plant?"

It was clear how prepared Vera and Henry had been for Red's arrival, as their downstairs bunker was completely equipped to be a self-contained flat. There was the main sitting room where the girls were sat. A kitchenette where Vera had made the tea and coffee. A bedroom with two single beds, in case Red had arrived with another cellmate as the elderly couple predicted. And a small bathroom that had only a toilet, sink and a narrow shower.

Vera turned to Trip, her expression revealing that she still couldn't quite believe what she was about to say:

"It was very bizarre. Ivan often encourages members of our family to go and visit that dreadful place. To show it off I guess. It's his pride and joy.

"One day, Henry took him up on the offer – purely out of curiosity. He'd been behind a screen with Carmen when you were all lining up for your scans. He caught a glimpse of Red's striking green eyes that we'd heard so much about from her mother, and had this strange feeling that it was her. I bided my time, before finally deciding to come and see for myself. I brought the map with me just in case. Looks like it was meant to be."

Vera smiled to herself, then wished the girls goodnight before leaving the underground bunker and making her way upstairs.

So far, everything seemed to have gone as planned for Vera and Henry, although it was unclear what would happen next. Did the elderly couple have a plan for this too?

I sure hope so, Trip thought to herself as she finished her last drop of coffee. It was only just starting to dawn on her that it was morning, meaning the guards would have most probably found the dummies in their cell. Have the alarms been rung already? How long would it be before Authorities came banging on the door of every house in the New Overworld?

These thoughts hadn't even flickered across Red's mind yet. All she could do was play Vera's words over and over again inside her head until they lost all meaning:

"Yes, dear. Your mother is dead."

"Yes, dear. Your mother is dead."

"Your mother is dead."

"Your mother is dead."

"…mother is dead."

"…dead."

It turned out that one day Red's mother had finally decided to stand up to Ivan Spencer. She was tired of asking him when he would be bringing her daughter up to the New Overworld with them and had decided she would go down to The Shell to find her.

Vera explained how she'd heard from other members of the family that this decision had led to a string of disagreements between the pair, before ultimately Ivan Spencer had Red's mother killed.

It was unclear how he had gone about doing this, but from what Vera had said, killing her had sent ripples throughout the family and the New Overworld. Red's mother was loved by the community. Vera spoke about what a warm and loving person Red's mother had been, despite the constant state of fear she lived in for her daughter's safety. Despite the sadness she felt for losing her husband. And the disgust she felt for being forced into a relationship with Ivan Spencer.

Trip reached her arm out to Red and placed it softly on her shoulder.

"I know you don't wanna 'ear this, Red. But we really should get some rest. We've got a lot to discuss and plan today."

Red simply pulled her shoulder away and said nothing.

Trip nodded to say she understood. "Imma leave you be now. I'll be in the bedroom if you need me." Trip then took herself to bed, where she fell into a deep sleep within minutes.

Red remained in a heap on the sofa, until she too passed out through utter emotional exhaustion.

* * *

Ethan stepped out of the transportation vessel into the arrival bay of the New Overworld. He felt the same shiver run down his spine as Red and Kyan had experienced before him. While the therapist was far more prepared for what he was about to see, the sight of the world untouched by a supposed asteroid was equally as shocking.

Ethan kept quiet as he followed Eric Vineyard past the concrete greys of the arrival bay. The first thing he noticed was the amount of children everywhere carrying guns and dressed as Authorities. Aged anywhere between six and eighteen, both boys and girls patrolled the area alongside Authorities twice their age. The only way to distinguish their gender was by the slight variation in uniform to reflect their physicality. Their Authority masks hid their youthful faces.

Although seeing violence among kids was nothing new in The Shell, there was something far more shocking about seeing these children in the New Overworld carrying weaponry. Ethan realised it was the fact it was under the command of adults. Violence was being encouraged by the very people who should have been protecting the kids.

Ethan bit his tongue and continued to follow his commander through the long tunnelled entrance to the New Overworld. To keep his hopes high, he kept Red's face securely in the forefront of his mind.

She's alive, she's alive, he repeated in his thoughts. *She just has to be alive.*

Red was very much alive. Although during the past five or six hours, she felt like she'd died. The news of her mother's death had broken something inside her that she knew would never be fixed again. But as she opened her eyes from a restless sleep, filled with nightmares of strangled angels, her sorrow had been replaced with anger.

First at her mother. How had she let all this happen? How had she just remained quiet as Ivan Spencer forced her into a relationship and killed Red's father? How had she allowed her daughter to be sent down to The Shell while she lived up in the New Overworld? A decision that had led Red into a life of danger and bad choices.

What if the vision Red had preserved of her mother for so long as a kind, warm and gentle human being had been wrong? What if it had all been a lie?

Perhaps her mother had wanted to be with Ivan Spencer. Perhaps she hadn't cared whether Red's father had lived or died and perhaps she'd wanted Red to be left in the United Underworld so she could focus on starting a new life.

Her anger quickly shifted from her mother back to Ivan Spencer as she reminded herself how this wouldn't have been the case. She knew her mother was a good person. Not only did she treasure the warm memories she had of her inside her heart, despite how faint they were becoming, but she'd seen first-hand the evil Ivan Spencer was capable of. And if he were able to convince an entire government to move humanity under the ocean while a new race was created over ground, then he definitely would have been able to convince her mother to leave Red in The Shell for what he would have described as safety.

It was also at that moment it truly dawned on Red that Ivan Spencer knew who she was. He had always known. Perhaps that's why she was able to run her underground bookstore for so long without being caught? Had her mother made him swear to keep her alive? Red winced as she remembered her bookstore being destroyed and Marcus dying. Had Ivan Spencer played a part in all this too? Had they all just been games?

She also winced as she wondered if this had all been part of his plan. To have her leave The Shell and be trapped in The Plant, simply used to produce children that would end up marching in his armies. Red's anger turned to determination once more as she thought of her daughter, being kept captive in The Plant in a similar way she was kept in The Shell.

"It's time to break this cycle," she finally said out loud.

The noise woke Trip up, who had been snoring heavily.

"You alrigh', love?" her croaky voice asked.

"I'm fine," Red replied bluntly. "It's time we end this battle, once and for all."

Trip sat up and smiled, wiping her eyes.

"Now that's the Red I know and love."

The pair jumped up and began to devise a plan, which began with Red realising that Vera and Henry must have connectors. Which meant she had to get in touch with Ethan and let him know she was alive.

* * *

"What's your name?" Ethan asked the boy. It was hard to work out his age seeing as his face was covered by an Authority mask, but judging by his height he can't have been much older than nine.

"My name is Zak," the boy answered with an unnerving tone that was mildly intimidating.

Ethan had been given permission to explore the almost derelict streets of the New Overworld for an hour as Eric

Vineyard met with officials inside the Government building, known as The Cloud. This is where Ivan Spencer and his right-hand officials lived.

A lone Authority remained with Ethan as he slowly paced around the New Overworld, although he had given him enough distance to begin a conversation with the boy called Zak.

"How long have you been… an Authority?" Ethan asked, lowering his voice slightly so the older Authority would not hear him.

"For as long as I can remember," Zak replied.

It dawned on Ethan that this kid was a child of the New Overworld. Born into lies. *Who knows what lies he has been fed about history*, he wondered. "And do you like being an Authority?" Ethan asked. This time there was about ten seconds of silence.

"Well, I…" the boy started. "I've never really given much thought to whether I like it or not."

It occurred to Ethan that he had struck a chord with Zak's psyche. His training as a therapist was paying off at a time when he needed it the most.

Ethan felt a slight buzz in his pocket as the message from Red reached his connector.

Slowly, keeping an eye on the older Authority who was stood using his own connector, Ethan reached down to slide the device from his pocket. He placed a finger on his lip to tell Zak to remain quiet. He knew he was taking a risk, seeing as he wasn't sure whether he had built enough trust with the boy yet, but it was one he was willing to take.

From an unknown number, Ethan read the words quickly:

ETHAN, IT'S RED. I'M ALIVE, I'M SAFE, I'M IN THE NEW WORLD. FOR WHAT IT'S WORTH, HERE'S THE ADDRESS: 85 ROCKDALE STREET, SUBURB 5, TNO 3420.

Fireworks exploded inside Ethan's heart.

Red was alive! She was really alive. After all this time. All the waiting. Guessing, hoping, secretly knowing but never wanting to say it out loud in case it jinxed it. Red was alive. And possibly within mere metres from where he stood.

Ethan slipped the connector back inside his pocket and grinned at the boy, before mouthing the words *thank you*.

"I hate it," Zak then said, in answer to Ethan's previous question. "But there's no other way."

Ethan shook his head.

"That's where you're wrong, son," he said. "Pass me the gun."

Zak paused for a few moments. This time it was his turn to be unsure whether he could trust his new acquaintance. But just like Ethan, what did he have to lose?

The boy passed Ethan the gun.

TWENTY-THREE

Without a second thought, Ethan shot a bolt of energy from the raygun straight into the older Authority's chest. The man let out a loud cry before falling to the floor. His body stuttered a few times and then went still.

This was his chance. His turn to be brave and strong. To do what was right in place of what he was ordered to do. Just like Red. The flames of her rebellion and defiance had burned strong inside Ethan's heart as he fired the shot.

Ethan moved quickly over to the dead Authority and began removing his uniform. He was relieved the bolt of energy from the raygun was able to kill the man without damaging what he was wearing. This was how the lethal energy worked. It would be absorbed into human flesh without leaving a cut or bruise. Zak stood in silence, just watching the scene play out in front of him. He felt no fear. His life had been built upon uncertainty and violence, so what he was witnessing felt like nothing new.

As Ethan had suspected, Zak was a child of the New Overworld. He was born in The Plant less than a year after the asteroid hoax had taken place, not that he remembered. He had been taken away from his mother straight away, just like all the other children from The Plant, and moved into a ward where he was cared for by nurses up until the age of five. This was the age when children would begin their training to join the army. By six he was patrolling the entrance to the New Overworld, with his raygun in hand.

"Come on," said Ethan. "I need you to take me to this address." Fully dressed in the Authority uniform, Ethan held his connector up to Zak to show him the message. The boy stood for a few moments, before nodding and leading the way. The dead man was left lying on the ground.

Ethan followed Zak through the gridded streets of the New Overworld. The large pastel-hued houses stood beside each other with neatly-manicured lawns out front. The sky was a light blue colour, doused in white fluffy clouds. It looked beautiful. Ethan found himself looking upwards beyond the large houses and the temple-like buildings behind them to the wonder of the open sky.

He hadn't allowed himself to appreciate the exquisiteness of the sky yet. It was not only something he hadn't seen for such a long time, but something he had never marvelled at or appreciated the way he did in this moment. As a child he had taken it for granted. He hoped that Zak didn't.

The clouds above and the fresh air on his face felt like a gift. A gift he was glad to be experiencing, particularly if he was going to be caught any minute by Eric Vineyard and his henchman and shot on the spot. Or worse, brought in front of Ivan Spencer to decide his fate.

But the thought of all the other citizens living in The Shell kept him going. It wasn't fair that they weren't going to get to experience the same simple luxuries ever again. Fresh air on their faces. Natural light. Ethan was determined to fight until they did.

The thought of finding Red also kept him going. Not only had she survived escaping The Shell before anyone else, but she'd managed to keep herself alive. If she'd managed to do that all this time, surely he could survive a couple of hours.

Ethan continued to follow Zak along the marble pavement. He felt sick to the stomach at the contrast of this world compared to The Shell. All of the space. So much room for the many people currently squashed together in the United Underworld. Like cockroaches. Piled together, climbing over each other.

The pair walked past a couple of Authorities patrolling the area, but neither paid them any attention. Ethan knew this meant the dead Authority hadn't been discovered yet, but this wouldn't last long. They would be coming for them any moment, so they would need to get to the address as soon as possible.

As if Zak had heard his thoughts, he stopped and instantly turned around before whispering:

"We're nearly there. Just two more blocks."

In this same moment, Red stepped out of the shower and began to pat her bruised and cut skin down. The water had felt heavenly against her ivory skin. She hadn't experienced a shower like that since her childhood. The water pressure in The Shell was weak and showers in The Plant had been even worse. So Red had allowed herself to take her time getting washed.

She'd imagined she was washing away all of the darkness from her skin. All of the pain and suffering. All of the time spent imprisoned. The news she'd just learned about her mother. Washed it all away. Set it free.

As she stepped out onto the soft carpeted floor, Red imagined herself being reborn. Clean of all the injustice. Clean of all the lies. Ready to start over. Stronger than ever before.

Once dried, she slipped into a silky robe that Vera had given her, which felt delicate and luxurious against her tired and broken skin. She looked into a mirror and couldn't believe the face that stared back at her. There were no mirrors in The Plant, so it had been a very long time since she'd seen her reflection. She wished she hadn't.

Her face was so gaunt it looked almost skeletal. The bags underneath her eyes were dark, adding to her skull-like appearance. It was easy to imagine her face without eyeballs, leaving just hollow dark sockets.

Her skin had always been pale during her time living in The Shell, but by this point it had a grey-like hue. She looked ill and defeated. The only hope of an appearance she once held was the short sprinkling of red hair that was quickly growing since her scalp had last been shaved.

Her moment of shock and self-loathing was interrupted by Trip's voice yelling through the door:

"He's 'ere, Red! Ethan's 'ere!"

Blood rushed through Red's veins like rain through drainpipes during a thunderstorm. Could it really be him? After all this time. All these days, weeks, months apart. Is he really here? She'd sent the message to him purely to let him know that she was alive. She thought she owed him that much after what she'd done to him. How, in less than an hour after giving him her address, could he already be here?

After Red lunged out of the bathroom and down the hallway, she froze in her tracks. What if Ethan was angry? After all, he had every right to be. If she hadn't acted on impulse and left her therapist tied up in his flat, would any of this have even happened? Would she have ended up in this situation?

Before she had time to contemplate these thoughts any longer, Ethan entered the hallway. Her heart went still.

It was as if no time had passed. His skin. Body. Hair. Presence. All just as they had been when she'd left him. Red on the other hand, was a different story. She was a shadow of her former self and had no idea how Ethan would react.

Still without a word being spoken, the pair started walking towards each other through the hallway. Like a magnetic force pulling them together at the very same time. And finally, following everything that had happened between Red drugging Ethan and leaving him tied up on his bathroom floor to this moment, the pair embraced. A warm, tight embrace.

Tears streamed down both Red and Ethan's faces. They barely noticed Trip, Vera, Henry and Zak standing behind them at the other end of the hallway.

"I'm sorry…" Red started to say, but Ethan stopped her.

"Shhh… don't be. We're here now, aren't we?"

With that, Red smiled and then started to laugh. First a quiet chuckle, before it transformed into full-blown hysterics. This triggered Ethan to do the same, followed by their audience of four. And just like that, a house filled with fear and sadness turned into a house filled with joy and laughter. But how long would it last?

In that very same moment, Eric Vineyard and his officials were discovering the body of the dead Authority. The general's face dropped as they approached the man, lying motionless in his underwear. It took Eric mere moments to piece together in his mind what had happened.

"Sound the alarms!" he cried out, his vein bulging out the side of his neck as he did so. "I want you all to scout every house, every street and every corner of woodland in the New Overworld until you find him!"

Authorities scattered off in different directions as the loud, throbbing and piercing sound of the alarms echoed throughout the New Overworld.

TWENTY-FOUR

Back in The Shell, Delta and Xavier's army had begun to grow even larger. The group was not only comprised of hundreds of citizens, but an increasing amount of Authorities who had decided there was no hope left for their own futures and were providing weapons, technology and transport to the army of rebels.

While Ethan had told Delta and Xavier to keep the army calm until they heard from him, the army itself had grown tired of waiting.

"We can't stand around down here, twiddling our thumbs," called out an ex-Authority to the army's leaders. Delta and Xavier had called a meeting in their secret headquarters to discuss the impatience they could feel arising from the rebels.

"What if your friend never comes back?" the man continued. "We'd be waiting forever. Or until Ivan Spencer decides to stop feeding us power down here." The masses of people surrounding the ex-Authority were nodding their heads and calling out in agreement.

"We understand your concerns," said Delta. "But we must remain calm. Ethan has a bigger plan for us all so we just need to be patient…" Before she could continue, one of the rebels shouted out:

"The time is now! The time is now!"

Other rebels joined in, "The time is now! The time is now! The time is now!"

Within moments, all of the rebels were chanting and beginning to march towards the exit of the headquarters. One of them had set a plank of wood on fire and was thrusting it in the air.

Xavier wrapped his arms around Delta, as the pair realised there was nothing they could do to stop the army.

"Perhaps they're right," Delta said. "Maybe the time really is now? After all, how long can we stand around and wait for Ethan to reappear when the likelihood of his survival seems so slim?"

Just as the rebels began spilling out onto the streets of The Shell carrying both burning torches and their weaponry, Ivan Spencer was being notified of Ethan's escape in the New Overworld. He called Eric Vineyard into his office.

"How on earth did you let this happen?" Ivan Spencer asked directly. His voice was icy and his face appeared even more gaunt than normal, as if he'd been consuming less than the small amount he already ate.

"We're still working on finding out exactly how this happened," Eric Vineyard said, slightly tripping over his words.

There weren't security cameras in the streets of the New Overworld, as Ivan Spencer hadn't anticipated the arrival of any escapees from The Shell. As for keeping an eye on the very few citizens of the New Overworld, his team could simply monitor their connectors. He was immensely regretting the decision not to have more surveillance devices installed.

"But of course it won't take long for us to find him, President," Eric continued. "It's not as if there's anywhere he can run."

Before Ivan Spencer could open his mouth to reply, Han Eden came running into the room.

"Sir, they're fighting back!" he cried out, trying to catch his breath after rushing to break the news. "The United Underworld is fighting back!"

Ivan Spencer's grey eyes opened wide, like two flying saucers. A venomous look swept across his face as he bit his lip for a few moments. Somewhere deep down inside he'd always known this day would come. Which is why he was prepared. Regaining his composure and slowly running his withered hand through his wispy white hair, he drew a deep breath before finally calling out three shrill words:

"Release the missiles."

Within the next ten minutes, Ivan Spencer's officials were carrying out their orders. They had received special training in preparation for this attack, which needed to be carried out with accuracy and precision.

Eric Vineyard entered the control room with the three most highly-trained officials in the New Overworld. He had wanted to focus entirely on searching for Ethan, but Ivan Spencer needed him to oversee the attack on The Shell. He'd sent two small groups of Authorities out to begin the search, one group patrolled the streets and the other was out in the forest.

"Now remember, we need to be careful and selective with our attacks," Eric said. "As we all know, the Reactor is powering all the energy and resources in the Overworld. It's vital that it remains intact."

The officials nodded in unison, before taking their stations to prepare for attack. Their first target was an abandoned industrial site near the area the rebels were marching. They weren't planning to kill anybody, just shock and scare them. The abandoned warehouses would be no loss to Ivan Spencer, but destroying them would send out a clear message. A reminder of who was in charge.

"Ready… aim… fire!" Eric spat out to the officials. Moments later, a large thin silver missile was shot from the artificial sky of the United Underworld and sent hurtling down towards the abandoned industrial site. A roaring explosion bellowed out across the district as the derelict buildings came crashing down in a pile of fire and rubble.

Delta screamed and fell forward. Xavier quickly reached out and caught her.

"I've got you!" he said.

"What was that!?" a member of the army called out. Delta and Xavier were with a group of seven people who had chosen not to leave the headquarters. The nine of them instantly ran outside their hideout, carrying their weapons with them.

Thick black smoke was quickly filling the surrounding streets of where the missile had been dropped. Delta coughed twice before covering her mouth and shutting her eyes. She then removed her hand when the truth dawned on her.

"It was a message," she said blankly. "Come on, let's get back inside."

Meanwhile out on the streets, the chaos was only just beginning. Members of the army ran to the scene with hosepipes to put out the flames that were quickly spreading. They knew they were risking their lives, both because of the aggressive fire and the chance of more missiles being dropped, but they knew they had to do everything they could to protect their home.

Despite the hatred the citizens of the United Underworld felt towards The Shell by now, it was still their home. It wouldn't take much for the ageing structure to be destroyed from the inside, letting the ocean crash in and drowning everyone. They couldn't let this happen. Not when they knew the outside world stood as alive and beautiful as it ever had.

While the army of rebels struggled to put out the flames in The Shell, Red, Ethan and Trip had started making plans as to what they would do next. They knew their time was limited and that Authorities would arrive at the house soon to search it. Although Vera and Henry were part of Ivan Spencer's family, they didn't imagine for a minute that he wouldn't have his officials turn their home upside down to search for the rebels.

As an ex-military general, Henry owned a vast array of equipment and weaponry that would come in use for the trio, as well as Zak who would have no choice but to tag along. As much as Vera and Henry would have liked to have kept the young boy safe with them, they knew he would be found and his fate would be certain.

There was a high chance that the Authorities wouldn't find the hidden bunker in the elderly couple's home. Thanks to Henry's military background, he'd managed to construct it in a way that was as well hidden as possible. Behind a bookshelf wall that was so thick and soundproof you wouldn't hear a scream. It had made Red smile when she first saw the bookshelf, as it had instantly reminded her of the old bookstore she'd owned. The dusty old printed books had also reminded her of Marcus. She thought how well her old friend would have gotten on with the elderly couple.

But there was also still a chance the Authorities would be able to find the bunker. If not on their first search, then definitely their second. This was a risk that neither Vera, Henry, Red, Ethan nor Trip were willing to take. Too many lives were already at stake.

Red had spent as little time as possible filling Ethan in on everything that had happened, but there were certain details she just couldn't keep secret. The death of his sister had led him to break down in tears, even though he'd been preparing himself for the news for many years. He probably would have lost all motivation to keep going completely if it wasn't for the news of his daughter.

"So you're telling me that somewhere out there right now we have a little girl who is being kept captive by Ivan Spencer's daughter?" Ethan couldn't hide the confusion in his words. Underneath the shock and fear, Red heard glimmers of joy in his tone.

Ethan had always wanted to be a father one day. Like Red, he'd never really given the idea too much thought considering circumstances within The Shell. But secretly he'd held onto the hope that it would be possible. That the world would change into something he'd actually want to bring a child into. He'd never dreamed this is how it would actually happen.

But despite his disappointment in the way his child had been brought into the world, and the fact that he hadn't been there to witness it, he felt warm inside knowing that he had a daughter. His own flesh and blood. And despite never seeing her face, Ethan felt true love towards his little girl. And he knew that he would do anything and everything within his power to find her and keep her safe.

"Yes," Red replied simply. "That's exactly what I'm saying. I'm sorry, I…"

Ethan stopped her before she said anything else, this time pulling her close towards his face. The pair kissed. After everything they'd been through since seeing each other last, it was as if nothing mattered except how they felt towards each other and the fact they had a daughter to save.

"As lovely as this scene is t'watch," Trip said, causing the pair to swiftly end their embrace, "we've kinda got an evil dictator to overthrow. And a revolution to take place, y'know?"

Red and Ethan couldn't help laughing. Their friend was right. There really was no time to lose. They would need to disguise themselves as **High Authorities** and step out into the deadly streets of the New Overworld. But first, they had a plan.

It all stemmed from the information Vera and Henry had shared with the young rebels about where the power in the New Overworld was coming from. Like a light flickering inside Red's mind, she realised the only way to shut down Ivan

Spencer's world would be to destroy the one thing the people of The Shell had spent the last decade working on. The Reactor.

Once again using the connector Vera had given to Red, she punched in the digits of Delta's number from memory. *It's now or never*, she thought.

It has to be now.

TWENTY-FIVE

Delta read the message aloud to Xavier and the seven other rebels in the hideout:

"Delta, it's Red. We are all safe. But we've worked out what we need to do. We need you guys to destroy the Reactor. It's powering the New World and without it, Ivan Spencer and his army will be helpless. You need to do this now!"

Both Delta and Xavier stood in silence, stunned as the words began to sink in. The incredible structure they had spent so much of their lives building and working on. This is what powered the evil regime above? A sudden feeling of sickness overcame the couple as they thought back to all the years they had dedicated to maintaining the Reactor. All the while they were helping power the development of a better world above them they were never even going to be a part of.

Following a few whispered exchanges between a pair of middle-aged men standing towards the back of the room, one of the ex-Authorities put his hand up and said: "We'll do it."

Xavier and Delta looked over at the men, still in shock. It became instantly clear what the two men shared in common. A yearning to get back at a government that had kept them in the dark for so long. They had nothing left to lose.

"Ar-are you sure?" Xavier hesitantly asked. "You know what this'll mean…"

"Of course we do," said the other man. "We're willing to sacrifice our lives for the sake of humanity's future."

"On top of that," the other man started saying, "we'd do anything to piss off those stupid idiots."

Both Xavier and Delta's faces broke out into smiles. But their grins weren't going to last for long.

Outside, a giant plume of inky smoke was still rising from the wreckage, although the rebels had managed to put out most of the flames caused by the missile's blow. There were many citizens and ex-Authorities still running around the rubble when the second missile was dropped. This time, it was clear Ivan Spencer's regime wasn't worried about causing fatalities.

The missile shot through the clouds of black smoke and landed directly in the area the last missile had struck. An even louder explosion erupted from the collision, sending both debris and human body parts flying in different directions.

"Shit!" Xavier called out. "Another attack!" The young man went to run upstairs and outside to check the damage, but Delta stopped him.

"Xave, they're not going to stop until we stop them. We need to focus on the plan."

Xavier nodded in agreement as he realised that they would

be helpless until all power from the New Overworld was shut down. Both he and Delta then turned their eyes back towards the two ex-Authorities.

And then there was silence, for there was nothing more to be said. Just explosives of their own to be prepared. And a government to finally be brought to its knees.

* * *

Moments before Red, Ethan, Trip and Zak were about to say their goodbyes to the elderly couple, the noise of High Authorities arriving at the front door stopped them in their tracks.

"Quick, get back down in the bunker!" Henry whispered to the crew, sending them running speedily through the secret bookshelf door and down the ladder into their hideout.

Vera slowly walked towards the front door when the Authorities knocked again, this time louder and more aggressively.

"Hello?" the Chief Authority called out.

"Just coming!" Vera called through the door, before turning back one last time to check the coast was clear. She opened the door.

A group of five Authorities marched into the house without saying another word to Vera and began searching each room.

"Would anybody like a cup of tea?" Vera asked.

"No thanks, ma'am," the Chief Authority replied. "We trust you know why we're here."

"Why, yes of course," Henry chimed in. "We've heard all about that man who escaped. It's the talk of the town!"

The Authorities opened cupboards, looked under the bed and checked the loft. Nothing. Vera started to get worried that they would suss out the hidden bunker behind the bookshelf. It seemed almost too obvious.

"You don't really think that we would be hiding this man here, do you?" Vera asked, doing her best to hide the fear in her voice. "We are family to Ivan Spencer."

"We're aware of that," the Chief Authority replied abruptly. "As are many people in some way or another in the New Overworld. Look, we're just carrying out orders. We won't keep you much longer."

Throughout all this, Red, Ethan, Trip and Zak kept as quiet as humanly possible in their secret hideout. Each of them clutched a weapon, just in case they were discovered. Even though the walls were soundproof, they were afraid to even breathe too heavily. Red kept her hand over Zak's mouth to ensure he didn't make a sound through his nerves. She could feel the young boy shaking.

After a few more minutes searching the old couple's home, it appeared that the Authorities were finally ready to leave.

"Sir, there doesn't appear to be anyone here," one of the Authorities said to his commander. The Chief Authority nodded in agreement.

"You're right. Let's move on."

At that same moment, both Vera and Henry noticed that one of the other Authorities stood frozen, staring at the bookshelf. Vera felt a lump appear in her throat and her blood turn stone cold.

He's worked it out, she thought to herself. *This one's clever, he's clocked on.*

The other four Authorities hadn't noticed their colleague's

discovery as they had already begun walking towards the front door to leave. Henry just stood still, staring at the Authority. Wondering what he was going to do next.

To the elderly couple's surprise, the Authority gave a quick nod before turning around and following the other troops out.

Is that it? Vera asked in her head, still too afraid to speak out loud. *Is he letting us off? Surely he worked it out by the way he was gazing so intensely at the bookshelf…*

Finally, Henry broke the silence.

"Let's not question it right now. Let's go let the guys know they're safe. We can worry about that later."

As Vera and Henry climbed down the ladder into the bunker, a loud sigh of relief filled the room.

"Thank you. Thank you. Thank you!" Ethan repeated to the couple.

"Don't waste time with all that," Henry replied. "They'll be back soon enough once they realise you haven't turned up elsewhere. Ivan will turn the land upside down until you're found. As much as we'd love to keep you here, we're worried it'll be even more dangerous than what could await you out there."

The group then changed into Authority uniforms provided by the elderly couple and loaded as much weaponry and other supplies as they could carry. After thanking the couple one last time for everything they had done, Red and her small army set out into the streets of the New Overworld and began heading towards the forest.

This time, Red was after justice. This time she was after blood.

SHELL

* * *

Dusk had arrived in The Shell as the two ex-Authorities headed towards the core area of the Reactor. The district was being heavily patrolled.

The roll-out of the artificial sunset had begun, just like every night, with the lights being slowly dimmed. This created a warm glow over the dusty streets of the United Underworld. During this time, it almost looked like The Shell and its buildings were constructed from something more precious than the rusting grey alloy actually used. For an hour, everything was gold, before it was plunged completely into darkness.

Ray and Karn, the two ex-Authorities who had volunteered to give their lives to destroy the Reactor, were dressed in their old gear. The uniforms felt as familiar as a favourite pair of shoes. But wearing them now just didn't seem right. They no longer believed in what the white armour stood for.

They had gone to the Reactor that night for a very different reason. For revenge. For justice. To finally start making things right. It all began with their task, their part of the mission. It all began with their ending.

The two men walked quickly up to where two Authorities stood guarding the entrance of the Reactor.

"Yes?" one of the on-duty Authorities asked.

"We've been sent here on special orders," said Karn assertively. "It's imperative we go inside."

Karn and Ray immediately aroused suspicion with their large backpacks, which Authorities didn't normally carry.

"Who sent you?" the other Authority asked.

"Ivan Spencer," Ray replied impulsively.

"Lies," the Authority hissed in reply.

Without hesitating, Ray pulled his raygun up and began firing. Light flashed and sparks flew out in different directions as the bolts of energy shot at the two Authorities before they even had a chance to retaliate.

"Quick, go!" Ray called out as he began to run forward. Karn grabbed the dead Authority's generator room access card before following, dimly aware that more Authorities would be right behind them.

As the two men ran towards the core of the Reactor, they did their best to tell civilians still working inside to escape. They had accepted there would be some innocent lives taken, but they decided it was a small price to pay for all the lives they were going to save.

"Run! Get outta here!" Karn called out as he ran.

"Go! Go!" Ray yelled at workers in the opposite direction.

Civilians stood up in their worker uniforms, looking puzzled. Without giving it another thought, they each began to flee the Reactor. One by one. But it was too late for them all to survive. Karn and Ray needed to complete their task before more Authorities arrived and shot them dead on the spot.

It was as if the world stopped turning on its axis as Karn and Ray lunged forward towards their destination. The central generator of the Reactor. The heart. The epicentre. The eye of the storm.

When they worked as Authorities they had seen where the generator was kept, but they had never before seen the inside of the room. The generator itself was sunken into the ground and epic in scale. Cables connected countless industrial-sized circuit boards. Copper-coloured cogs turned as steam made the room unbearably hot. Although the generator was bigger than they had expected, they knew the explosives they had built would cause damage if they leapt directly into its mechanics.

As the two men plummeted into the generator carrying their lethal backpacks, they both spared one final thought for the world they were leaving behind. Imagining a new world that everyone was allowed to inhabit. Not just the one percent.

An enormous explosion propelled throughout The Shell. Both the United Underworld and the New Overworld were immediately plunged into darkness.

"They did it!" Delta called out into the rebels' headquarters, which had been filled with candles in preparation. Xavier and the rest of the army who had remained with them cheered in celebration. But their party spirit would not last long. They had a mission to carry out.

Now that the Reactor had been destroyed, the electromagnetic locks on the gates to the exit zone of The Shell would be deactivated. This meant the team could finally get to the vessels and escape.

Ivan Spencer turned around in his office, which was almost pitch black, lit only by a post-sunset glow through the windows.

"What's happened!?" he shrieked out into the corridor. Dozens of officials were running around with flashlights.

"President, we've lost connection with The Shell!" Eric Vineyard declared as he appeared, holding a torch. "Something must have happened to the Reactor!"

Ivan Spencer's face showed rage at first, before transforming into a look Eric had never seen his leader show before. Fear. Ivan Spencer was actually afraid.

"Well, what are you waiting for!?" the thin man spat. "Fix it!"

"We have a backup generator we're just powering up now to bide us some time while we set out to repair the Reactor," Eric replied. This time it was him who couldn't hide his fear.

"I don't care what you have to do to fix it," his leader responded. "Just do it!"

As Ivan Spencer called out his orders, Delta, Xavier and the rebels that were with them managed to catch up with the rest of their army at the departure gate of The Shell. Clutching fire torches to help them navigate through the darkness, the reunited group began cheering and hugging each other.

"C'mon!" called out Xavier. "We need to take this chance to head to the Overworld while the exit gates are unlocked!"

The army, which had once again grown large, began opening fire on the Authorities guarding the exit. Despite the fact that lives were lost on both sides, Xavier, Delta and many more of the rebels managed to climb into vessels and start heading towards the New Overworld. Xavier turned around to face his girlfriend.

"Are you ready for this?" he asked.

Delta smiled and nodded.

"Let's go get our girl."

As the rebels' vessels hurtled away from The Shell, Ivan Spencer was entering a vast room back on mainland where High Authorities stood in lines. Eric Vineyard had managed to use the backup generator to send power to the majority of The

Cloud, but this didn't extend to The Shell or The Plant. This meant the locks on the gates to both prisons were deactivated.

Dozens of officials were tapping on holographic screens as they tried to regain connection with The Shell. Ivan Spencer stood up in front of his troops and began to bark out orders.

"I always knew this day could come. The day the cockroaches of the Underworld would revolt. Well, it won't last long… we will defeat them. From this moment onwards, I declare war!"

The rows of High Authorities punched their hands into the air and cheered.

"War!" they echoed.

"Now I need every one of you out there on the ground! They have an army, but we outnumber them. I need the men, women and children armed and ready to attack as soon as they arrive! What are you waiting for? Go!"

The army of Authorities began running towards the exit of The Cloud, pumped up with adrenaline as they clutched onto their rayguns. They were ready to take no prisoners. They were ready to die in the name of their leader. They were ready.

TWENTY-SIX

The High Authorities began sprinting through the marbled streets towards the arrival bay, as the army of rebels were already climbing out of their vessels.

Authorities guarding the entrance were swiftly shot down by the rebels as they jumped out. Feeling the solid ground beneath their feet for the first time in years was enough to make them feel empowered. After they'd seen the world again, there was no way they were going to allow themselves to get killed. There was too much that was worth fighting for. Too much to lose.

While the rebels started to run through the arrival bay's unlocked gates, disappearing into its adjacent forest, Red, Ethan, Trip and Zak were drawing closer to The Plant which they could see was heavily guarded.

"There's no way we'll get past 'em," Trip said. "Not with jus' the four of us."

"We have to try," Red answered defiantly. "We've come this far now. They know the gates are unlocked so they're vulnerable. We just need to give the prisoners the sign that they can escape."

"But they're unarmed, Red," Trip replied. "They'll be shot down one by one if we do that."

As if their prayers had been answered, the army of rebels started to appear in the distance.

"Look!" Ethan cried out. "They've made it! They've actually made it here!"

The Authorities guarding the doors of The Plant noticed the rebels in the distance and began running towards them, opening fire.

"Quick!" Red shouted. "Now's our chance, run for it!"

As the army of rebels and the Authorities ran towards each other shooting blasts from their rayguns in all directions, Red, Ethan, Trip and Zak made a dash towards the doors of The Plant. Within moments, they were inside.

"Ok, guys," said Ethan. "This is it. Now, there's not many of us and we don't know how many Authorities will be in here. So we gotta stick together."

"There shouldn't be many," Trip replied. "Mainly guards, who'll be easy enough to get rid of. Look, 'eres one now!"

Trip shot a blast of energy towards a guard who had appeared around the corner, sending him flying backwards and hitting the floor with a loud thud.

The determined foursome then began running through the confined corridors of The Plant. While Red and Trip had explained the situation inside The Plant to Ethan, nothing could have prepared him for the sight of all the imprisoned pregnant women with shaved heads. Empty eyes looking out through the barred windows of their cell doors.

"Help! Help us!" one woman screamed.

"Don't tell them the doors are open," Red whispered. "It's not safe for them yet."

Three more guards ran through the door.

"Halt!" one of them yelled. "Who goes there?"

"Let 'em 'ave it!" Trip called out through her helmet. Flashes of light flickered as shots were fired on both sides.

Zak screamed in agony as a blast blew off his right hand, sending it flying with his weapon. He quickly ran for cover around the corner. Blood followed his path.

Red shot one of the guards in the back of the head as he ran after the young boy. The man fell to the floor and died instantly. The imprisoned women howled and cheered, rattling the bars on their cell doors.

It was only after Ethan shot two more men down that he realised he was also injured. A bolt of energy had hit him in his left shoulder and he could feel the blood seeping through his Authority uniform.

"Ethan, are you all right?" Red asked gently as she got down to kneel beside him. She removed her helmet and focused her eyes on her lover's wound. Ethan smiled. He then started to chuckle.

"What? What is it?" she asked.

"I've never seen you so compassionate," Ethan replied. "You've come a long way, Red."

Tears welled up in her eyes. Everything they'd been through

flashed before her. The first time Ethan had turned up at her home as her therapist. When they visited his favourite bar. The first time they kissed. When they made love.

Now here they were, after being so long apart, finally reunited and closer than ever to finding their daughter. Red wasn't prepared to let him die on her. She'd lost too much already. Too many people she loved.

"Come on, Ethan," she said. "You can do this. You have to, for our daughter…"

A look of determination came over Ethan's face.

"You're right," he said climbing back up onto his feet. "Let's do this."

"Do what?" Carmen asked, as Trip felt a raygun being held to the back of her head. Two guards stood either side of Carmen, also clutching weapons. Red recognised them instantly.

"Drop your weapons," Carmen said coldly. The stunned threesome had no choice but to oblige.

Carmen's hair was cut into a blunt bob and bleached so white it was almost grey. Her thick makeup was smudged around her eyes, revealing she'd been crying. This gave Red a glimmer of satisfaction, even though she was preparing herself to die.

"I should have killed you once you'd given birth to that little brat," Carmen said venomously.

"Screw you," Red spat without thinking.

Carmen laughed. "Looks like you haven't lost your charm. You know, I was pretty impressed that you girls managed to escape. No one has managed that before. Sure, women have tried. But I always caught them. I always shot them dead on the spot."

Trip gulped loudly.

"I guess it just took me a little longer to catch up with you both," Carmen continued. "But I'll take twice as much pleasure in killing you."

"Don't touch her," Ethan chimed in. "Either of them!"

Once again, Carmen let out a loud cackle. "And you must be the therapist everyone was searching for. I don't see what all the fuss is about, really."

Carmen looked Ethan up and down and then smiled. "I take it you're the father, no?"

Silence.

She then looked back at Red. "Follow me, I want to show you something." Carmen then led the way as the two guards followed behind, keeping their rayguns aimed at the three young rebels.

Red couldn't believe she was back in that place. A prisoner of The Plant once more.

As Red, Ethan and Trip were escorted into the control room, they were immediately greeted with visions of violence on huge screens.

"Your plan to take out the Reactor was very clever," Carmen said. "But foolish all the same. That piece of engineering that your people worked on for so long is now destroyed, meaning we're having to rely on a backup generator."

The screens showed live footage of what was taking place outside in the forest. Continuous flashes of light signalled the shots being fired between the army of rebels and the Authorities. Many people on both sides had lost their weapons and were fighting with their fists. They were punching and kicking. Some were even biting each other.

Piles and piles of dead bodies lay on the ground as the scorched trees and bushes burned beside them. Men. Women. Children. All dead as the battle continued. Military drones were capturing every moment and transmitting it back to The Plant in real time. At one point, Red caught a glimpse of Xavier and Delta, who were both hiding behind a tree trunk. Badly injured and dripping with blood.

She vomited.

Ethan wrapped his arm around Red, attempting to console his love.

Once again, Carmen's laugh echoed throughout the room.

"Touched a nerve, has it?" she asked wickedly. "But wait, the best is yet to come." She tapped a button and the footage changed to visions of The Shell. The warzone that once was Red and Ethan's home made the forest look like a paradise.

Mountains of dead corpses. Burning buildings and pods. Missiles being dropped every few seconds.

"Looks like daddy established connection with the Underworld again," Carmen said through her grin. "Meaning it will be locked, so no more people can escape. And, now that the Reactor's gone, he has no reason to hold back on attacking your filthy people."

Tears welled up in Red's eyes. "It's all my fault," she muttered quietly.

"No it's not!" Ethan quickly replied.

"She's right!" Carmen corrected. "That's exactly the point I wanted to get across to you before I kill you all. This is all your fault, Red. Now your people will die because of you. One. By. One."

Moments later, Zak came flying into the room opening fire with a newly acquired raygun. He had tightly wrapped fabric around his wrist to stop it from bleeding where his hand had been blown off.

His shots instantly killed both the two guards standing at the back of the room. Stunned, Carmen didn't have a chance to process what was happening before Red had swung her fist and knocked the gun out of her hand. She then quickly pulled a switchblade out from the inside of her boot and held it against Carmen's neck, clutching onto her bleached hair. Out of all the weapons Henry had, this was the one she'd been instantly drawn to. She'd missed her own switchblade far too much.

Red looked up to a security camera where she knew Ivan Spencer would be watching.

"Ceasefire, or I'll kill her!"

The screens automatically changed to show Ivan Spencer's evil face.

"Stop!" he said, visibly terrified. "Ok, I'll call for a ceasefire. Please don't kill her."

"How can I believe you?" Red asked pulling Carmen's hair tighter and holding the knife closer to her skin. Her neck started to turn red.

"Daddy! Help me!" she shrieked.

"I'll do it right now!" he said. "I'll do anything you want!"

"I want you to meet me outside," Red replied. "But call a ceasefire right now."

"Ok," Ivan Spencer replied, trying to remain calm. "Bring her outside now and I'll meet you there."

As the five of them began walking down the corridors of the prison, Red paused quickly, still clutching onto Carmen with the switchblade at her throat. She realised their doors would be locked again seeing as the backup generator was sending power to The Plant.

"I know you all hate this woman, but right now I need you to trust me and wait patiently in here where you will be safe," she called out to the prisoners. "We'll be coming back for you very shortly."

Outside, it was clear that the battle had been ground to a halt. Red wasn't sure how the message had been communicated so quickly, or why the rebels had agreed to stop fighting. But she was glad they had. By this point she just wanted peace. She was so happy to hear silence.

A chopping sound. Red looked up and saw a giant helipod flying down from overhead. He was coming. The man she'd loathed so much her entire life was actually on his way. She was finally going to be faced with him. Her breath grew rapid, matching Carmen's terrified short bursts. Red pulled the switchblade tighter against her neck.

"Keep quiet!" she ordered.

Ethan stood in silence in the background. He couldn't believe what he was witnessing, but he knew Red needed to do this on her own. As she'd always made clear, she didn't need rescuing. And this moment was no exception.

The helipod landed on the grass of the forest as the crowds gathered around trying to get a closer look at what was taking place. The army of rebels and Authorities circled the flying vehicle, leaving enough space for Red and her hostage.

The adrenaline that was pumping through Red's veins started to give way to a different feeling. Fear. What was she doing? She could be dead in a second with a single blast from one of Ivan Spencer's bodyguards' rayguns. Was it really worth risking this? She was finally reunited with Ethan and so close to finding her daughter. Was she really going to throw it all away?

But as Ivan Spencer began slowly pacing down the heli-pod's runway, escorted by Han Eden on one side and a High Authority on the other, Red's fear was once again overtaken by another emotion. Not just anger, but hatred. Everything that had happened to her between being separated from her mother and where she stood at this point flashed before her. Everyone she'd lost. All because of the evil dictator in front of her. It was like everything had led to this moment. And she was going to ensure she enjoyed it, whether she lost her own life in the process or not.

"I didn't want you to miss out on seeing this in real life," she said with words filled with malice.

"Kill her!" Ivan Spencer shrieked to his officials. But to both his and Red's surprise, the two men instead grabbed their leader by the arms and held him facing forward. Were they making him watch? Red quickly realised this was the case and was hardly surprised. The opportunity had finally come for the dictator to be overthrown and even his closest allies were ready to watch him crumble.

With great satisfaction, Red slit the throat of Ivan Spencer's daughter, right in front of his eyes. As she did this, she thought of both her parents and Ethan's sister. All dead because of Ivan Spencer's cruel actions. She wanted him to experience the same pain and loss as they had.

Gasps of shock rippled throughout the circle of onlookers. Dark red blood poured down across Carmen's body as she let out a piercing scream that transformed into a rattle.

"No!" Ivan Spencer called out into the night.

Red dropped the dead woman to the ground, still clutching on to her bloodied switchblade. The president, who had slumped back as far as he could go with the two tall officials holding his arms in a grip, opened his eyes. He'd kept them closed during the violent murder. Red could see tears welling up.

"Nothing will bring back all the lives you've taken," she said blankly. "But we're going to reverse all the damage you've done. Piece by piece." She bent down and scooped up a handful of dirt.

"This world doesn't belong to you any more." She then threw the grit into the old man's thin face, leading him to cough and splutter.

To the surprise of every onlooker, Red slid the switchblade back into the side of her boot. She then turned around, and simply said:

"Let the people decide his fate."

Within moments, crowds of people launched forward towards the withering man. Rebels. Authorities. Men. Women. Children. Everyone was pushing forward to get a piece of the dictator's brutal death.

Ethan, who had still been standing further back with Trip

and Zak, noticed Eric Vineyard pop his head out of the helipod to get a closer look at what was going on.

Without a second thought, the young man lifted his raygun up and aimed it directly at his old general. He pulled the trigger, sending a shot of energy hurtling forward and killing his opponent instantly. The blaze also caused a small explosion in the side of the helipod, sending it into flames. Anyone else left inside the vehicle wouldn't have stood a chance.

Trip then noticed Red had gone back inside The Plant.

"Quick," she said. "Let's go find your daughter."

The pair ran inside, while Zak joined the huge crowd of people who had circled Ivan Spencer. As the young boy weaved his way through the crowd and got closer to the gory centre, his blood ran cold at the sight of what was in front of him. Han Eden was holding the dead dictator's head in the air as if it was a trophy. The blood still pouring out onto the floor.

TWENTY-SEVEN

Trip and Ethan ran through the constricted corridors of The Plant, searching for the room where Trip remembered the babies were taken. Although neither of them said it, they were both terrified of what they could find. Would Carmen have killed the children in a rage before they found her? They both shuddered at the thought. Women called out through their cell doors on both sides of the corridor.

"We need to get these women outta 'ere," Trip said. "You go ahead and find Red. Take two more lefts and then you'll find the door on th' right."

Ethan nodded, then continued on. As he ran, he could feel his heart pounding in his chest and the sweat beginning to trickle down his back. Could this really be happening? Was he really going to meet his child for the very first time? He hadn't even been aware of her existence very long, so the fact he could soon be holding her was beyond surreal.

But what if his fears were right? What if it really was too late? Ethan blocked these thoughts out of his mind as he took the second left and saw the door at the end of the corridor on the right.

"She's in there!" a woman shouted out through the window of her cell door. "Red said she'd be back for us. And she kept her word!" The woman sounded half ecstatic and half insane.

Ethan said nothing. He drew a large breath in, filling his lungs with air, then ran forward. *It's now or never.*

As Ethan burst through the unlocked door, he felt a wave of euphoria at what he saw in front of him. In a room filled with babies, some crying and some asleep, Red stood holding their child. Rocking slightly side to side, Red opened her eyes and smiled in a way Ethan had never seen her smile before. For the first time in the whole time he had known her, Red looked truly content.

"Come meet our daughter," she said softly.

Tears welling up inside his eyes, Ethan walked over quickly and embraced his two greatest loves. Suddenly, everything was right in the world. Finally they were complete.

Meanwhile, Trip had managed to find the control room of The Plant. Her eyes darted across the screens as she tried to familiarise herself with what it all meant. She began tapping and swiping on a screen until she was met with three words: Disarm All Locks.

Just when she thought it wasn't possible to feel any more excitement in one hour, she tapped the request twice, and a loud electronic voice blasted out throughout The Plant.

"All Locks Disarmed."

Hysteric cheers of elation filled the building as the pregnant prisoners of The Plant began pushing their cell doors open. Some running to find their babies, while others headed straight towards the exit. Ethan and Red quickly left the room they were in to catch up with Trip and watch the beautiful scene unfold.

Through the opened front doors of The Plant, the three friends watched hundreds of women running out into the cold night's air. Witnessing how blessed they all felt to finally be outside again, Red smiled as she thought of all the people inside The Shell who would soon be freed.

It was over. It was finally over.

* * *

Over the next few days, the residents of The Shell were transported back onto land. Vessel by vessel, the residents of the United Underworld were moved into the New Overworld, which had been given the new nickname: *The Free Land*.

But it would not be able to stay leaderless for long. New laws would have to be written and rules obeyed, to avoid more chaos and destruction. Many people wondered if Red and Ethan would step into the roles of leaders, but both quickly declined this suggestion. After everything they had been through, they were ready to live their lives as simply and peacefully as possible.

Both of them did play a part in appointing the new government though, which was to be made up of the army of rebels they had built in The Shell. With Delta and Xavier, who although were badly injured were recovering quickly, as the newly-appointed leaders.

A large open-air gathering took place a week after the death of Ivan Spencer and the inhabitants of The Shell had moved back onto land. Held in the forest where the final battle had taken place, a stage had been set up with the words *Welcome to the Free Land* written across it.

Red took to the stage after Ethan had finished speaking to the crowds of citizens standing in front. The ceremony was also being transmitted across the country, where redevelopments were already quickly underway.

Wearing a long flowing dress in a delicate blue hue that cut a striking silhouette across her slender figure, Red stood in front of the crowds and prepared to speak into the microphone. Her shaved head was looking far softer with her hair quickly growing through.

"I can't quite believe I'm standing here in front of you all today," Red began. The colour of the sky above mirrored the shade of her dress. Littered with a few clouds, the birds sang loudly signalling the start of spring. Red continued:

"There were many moments during my quest that I thought my time was up. Whether it was when I faced the brutal waves of the Atlantic when I escaped The Shell, or when my friend Trip and I climbed through the dingy sewers of the New Overworld to escape The Plant.

"It's been quite the journey to get to where I'm standing today... and it's not over yet. The real hard work begins now, with repairing our world and economies. With rebuilding a system that works, that is not flawed or corrupt. And it all begins with two of my oldest and dearest friends. Say hello to your new leaders, Delta and Xavier."

The crowds erupted into applause as the couple took the stage and gave their friend a kiss of gratitude. Xavier's arm was in a cast and Delta looked visibly cut and bruised. But their smiles outweighed all this. And the genuine love and goodness in their hearts signalled to the world exactly what sort of leaders they were going to be.

As Xavier and Delta took their places in front of the microphone to thank their friend and begin an introductory speech into what their plans for The Free Land were, Red walked off the stage and headed back to her seat in the front row. There she was met with Vera, Henry, Trip, Zak and Ethan, who was holding Pearl. The couple had called their daughter this in honour of Red's mother, who had shared the same name.

Despite everything that had happened, Red did not blame her mother for anything. She knew she'd had her reasons for leaving her in The Shell and that she'd lost her life in an attempt to save her. She knew that her mother had done everything she possibly could to have protected her daughter. Red was ready to do the same for Pearl.

Red took her seat next to Ethan and was quickly greeted by a plump black cat hopping onto her lap. She laughed at how big her old feline friend, Aura, had become. At least she knew she'd been well fed back in The Shell.

Red looked up and watched on with pride as her oldest friend spoke about her plans to lead The Free Land away from the darkness and into the light. She spared a thought at how far Delta had come. How far they all had come.

EPILOGUE

It was half a decade after the revolution had occurred, somewhere near the sea. A beautiful house stood on an otherwise isolated stretch of land, a stone's throw from the sand.

"Quick, mummy!" the young girl said. "I want to build another sandcastle!"

The girl ran across the grassy dunes that led to the sandy beach. Her auburn locks hung down across her freckled face.

Her mother walked slowly in a light ivory dress. Her long red hair tied into a thick side plait. Barefoot, she followed her daughter towards the crashing waves. Her pregnant stomach only partially visible.

Once sat down, the woman noticed a single shell lying in the otherwise clear sand. Like the isolated home that stood behind them. She picked it up and smiled to herself.

"Darling, I want you to hold this against your ear. Inside, you will hear the ocean."

SHELL

The young girl took the shell into her small and delicate hands, before obeying her mother's words. A look of wonder and amazement. As if it was magic.

Then, the girl moved the shell away from her ear, stood up again and stared out towards the waves. As if in a trance. She looked back up at her mother, this time her crystal green eyes filled with curiosity and determination. It was a look her mother knew only too well.

Seagulls squawked above, the same way they always did. Distant caws that would forever evoke nostalgic childhood memories. Circling in the same way time does. An infinite loop that can never be broken.

ABOUT THE AUTHOR

Chris Gill spent time growing up in both England and New Zealand, studied journalism at university in Hampshire and worked as a copywriter in London. He has released both a book of poetry and a memoir through his co-founded publishing company, PRNTD, and contributed articles to websites and magazines around the world. He now lives in Sydney, Australia.

Twitter @ChrisWGill

www.chrisgillbooks.com

Lightning Source UK Ltd.
Milton Keynes UK
UKOW02f0101241116
288390UK00001B/37/P